George Manville Fenn

The New Forest Spy

George Manville Fenn

The New Forest Spy

ISBN/EAN: 9783337320485

Printed in Europe, USA, Canada, Australia, Japan

Cover: Foto ©Andreas Hilbeck / pixelio.de

More available books at **www.hansebooks.com**

THE NEW FOREST SPY

BY

GEO. MANVILLE FENN

LONDON

JOHN F. SHAW & CO. LTD.,

3 PILGRIM STREET, LUDGATE HILL, E.C.

CONTENTS

I L L U S T R A T I O N S

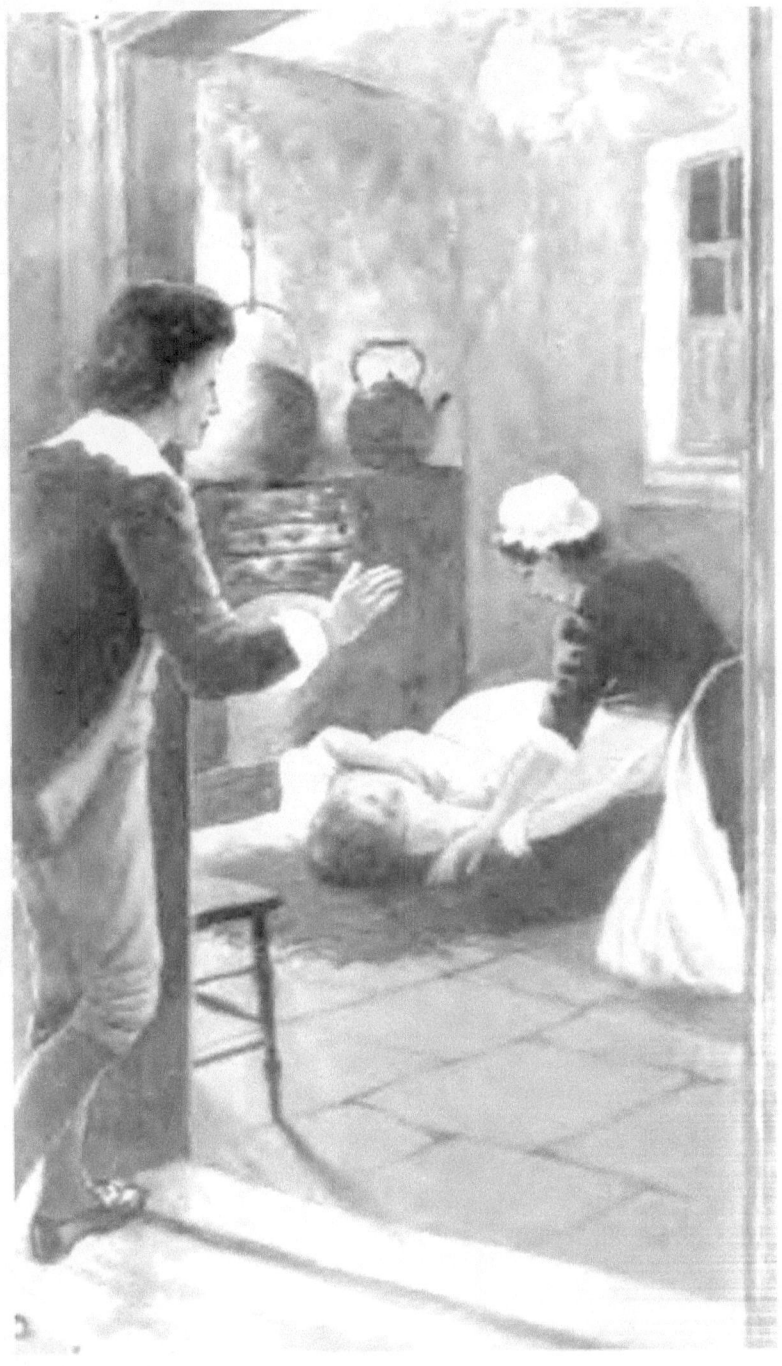

THE
NEW FOREST SPY

CHAPTER I.

AN ENCOUNTER IN THE WOOD.

" Hullo ! What's that ? "

The lad who uttered those words dropped a short, stiff fishing-rod in amongst the bracken and furze, and made a dash in the direction of a sharp rustling sound to his right, ran as hard as he could, full-pelt, for about five-and-twenty yards, and then, catching his toe in a tough stem of heather, went headlong down into a tuft of closely-cropped furze— the delicate finer kind—which had been nibbled off year after year till it had assumed the form of a great green-and-gold cushion, beautiful to look at, but too pointed in its attentions to make a pleasant resting-place.

" Bother ! " shouted the boy, as he scrambled up. " Oh, what an ass I am ! Anyone would think I was old enough to know that I couldn't catch a rabbit on the run, even if

he had no hole among the hazel-stubbs.
Hole ? Hundreds, where he could dive down.
Horrid, prickly things furzes are. That was
a sharp one ; but there, it hasn't hurt much,
only it makes one so jolly hot."

He walked backward along the edge of the
forest much more deliberately to stoop and
pick up his rod.

" Yes, of course," he grumbled, and he
screwed up a rather good-looking young manly
face into a grin of annoyance which shewed
all his closely set white teeth ; " I might have
known—all in a tangle. The hook broken,
of course ! "

He let the butt of the rod which bore a very
old-fashioned brass winch, rest in the hollow
of his arm, while he carefully extricated the
hook at the end of his line from where it had
fallen and caught hold of a stem of dwarf
bracken, while to free it and the hair, feather,
and dubbing which had transformed the said
hook into what was supposed to be a big
artificial fly, although it was not in the
slightest degree like any insect that ever flew,
required no little care.

" Humph ! " he grunted ; " might have
been worse. But what a stupid a trout must
be to go at a thing like that ! Well, so much

the better for me. Now then : once more, to begin."

But the boy seemed in no hurry to start. His exertions, though slight, had made him very hot, and he took off his cap to wipe away the shining drops that covered his sun-tanned forehead and stood thickly where, higher up, the skin was white amongst the thickly set curls of his brown hair.

He looked round at a common-like portion of the New Forest over a slightly undulating stretch of velvety grass, bracken, heather and stunted oak-trees, which gave the place a park-like aspect, running right up to where the oaks were clustered thickly, with an occasional silvery or ruddy barked birch, and made dense with hazel stubs and alder.

" Oh, what a jolly day ! " he said ; " but isn't it hot ! "

It was, for the autumn sun shone down out of a vivid blue sky upon the gloriously green growth which was beginning here and there to look mellow and ripe as if shot with ruddy gold.

" I might just as well lie down and read under the shade of one of the trees," mused the boy, " for the trout will be all in the most cranky places right under the stones and roots.

But one can't read without a book, and I came out on purpose to catch something, and I mean to do it ; so here goes."

He made for the nearest portion of the forest, and plunged in at once, holding his fly carefully between finger and thumb, and shouldering his rod so that, as he walked on with the trees clustering thicker and thicker, he drew the top after him, and got on fairly well without entangling his line.

Deeper and deeper into the forest, which grew more and more dense, till, breaking away from its level, it suddenly began to descend in a stiff slope, which rose as steeply fifty yards farther on, forming in all a wandering, tangled little valley, at the bottom of which trickled and gurgled a tiny river some few yards wide, flashing brightly in places where the sun passed through the overhanging trees, but for the most part darkly hidden, and only to be approached with some little difficulty and at the risk of being caught and held by one of the briars' hundred hands.

The valley was very beautiful, gloriously attractive, and evidently a very sanctuary for blackbirds, one of which every now and then darted out in full velvet plumage, skimmed a few yards, and then dived out of sight again.

They were too common objects to take the boy's attention as he cautiously made his way towards the edge of the little river, but he did stop for a minute as a loud *yuk*, *yuk*, *yuk*, rang out, and a good-sized bird made a streak of green, and, once well in the sunshine, of brilliant scarlet, as it flew over the bushes and amongst the trees in a series of wave-like curves before it disappeared.

" That's the greenest woodpecker and the reddest head I have seen this season," said the boy thoughtfully. " That's a fine old cock-bird, and no mistake. Well, green woodpeckers aren't trout, and he wouldn't take my fly if I dropped it near him, and I don't want him to. Now, then, what do you say to a try here ? "

The lad asked himself the question, and responded by going on cautiously for about a dozen yards through about the most unsuitable pieces of woodland possible for a fly-fisher to try his craft.

But Waller Froy, only son of the Squire of Brackendene, was not going to wield a twelve-foot fly-rod, tapering and lissom, and suitable for sending a delicate line floating through the air to drop its lure lightly on the surface of the water. Such practices would have been utterly impossible on any part of the woodland rivulet. But, all the same, he knew perfectly well what he was about, and how to catch the large, fat, dark-coloured, speckled beauties that haunted the stream—the only way, in fact, unless he had descended to the poacher-like practice of " tickling," and that he scorned.

Waller's way was to proceed cautiously through the undergrowth without stirring bough or leaf till he came to some opening on the bank where he could see the dark, slowly gliding stream, or perhaps eddy, through the overhanging boughs.

Then, with his fly wound up close to the top ring of his short rod, he would pass it through the leaves and twigs with the greatest care and unwind again, letting the fly descend till it dropped lightly on the surface. This he did patiently in fully a dozen different places, winding up after each attempt, and then cautiously following the edge of the stream to try again wherever he came upon a suitable spot. But upon that particular occasion the trout were not at home at the lairs he tried, or else not hungry, so the fly was drawn up again for fresh trials.

" It's too hot," muttered the boy.

But he had all the good qualities of a fisherman, including patience and perseverance, and he went on and on deeper and deeper into the forest, managing so skilfully that he never once entangled his line.

It was very beautiful there in the soft shades. The sun was almost completely shut out, and in some of the openings the pools looked absolutely black, while Waller, perfectly confident that there were plenty of good pound trout lurking in this hiding-place of theirs, went on and on.

· He had left the outskirts of the forest far behind, threading the rugged oaks, to make his way through the undergrowth that flourished amongst the beeches—huge forest monarchs that had once been pollarded by the foresters of old, to sprout out again upon losing their heads into a cluster of fresh stems, each a big tree—so ancient that, as the boy gazed back at them from where he wound his way in and out, following the curves and zigzags of the little river, he asked himself why it was that this tract of land was called the New Forest, where everything looked so old.

" How stupid ! " he muttered, the next
moment. " I forgot. Of course, it was because William Rufus made it for hunting in.
It was new then if it isn't now. I wonder
whether he ever fished for trout," added the
boy, with a laugh. " Good thing for him if he
had ; people who go fishing don't often get
shot. Ah ! there ought to be one here."

The denseness of the briars and wild-rose
tangles had forced him to make a *detour*, and
now, on drawing near the river again, he
came upon so likely a spot that, practising
the greatest caution, he dropped his big ugly
fly through what was quite a hole in the
overgrowth of verdure, beneath which the
water lay still and dark.

He was quite right. He felt that there ought
to be a fish there waiting for some big fat
caterpillar or fly to drop from the leaves above;
and his ugly lure had hardly touched the
surface of the water before there was a loud
smack, a disturbance as if a stone had been
thrown in to fall without a splash, and a well-
hooked trout was darting here and there at
the end of the short line, making frantic
struggles to escape.

But though Waller Froy had so many yards
of twisted silk upon his winch for the con-

venience of lowering and winding-in his bait, the tangle of bushes and overhanging boughs necessitated fishing with a tight line, with trust in its strength for the rapid hauling out of the prize.

It was no question of skill, but the roughest of rough work ; and after a few rapid plunges and splashes, the fish was lifted out on to the bank, to begin leaping and making the first steps to entangle the line amongst the twigs which rose everywhere about the boy's knees.

" What a beauty ! " he cried, as he released his hook, placed his prize in his creel, and proceeded to examine his ruffled fly, getting it ready for tempting another fish.

This was tried for in a similar place about a dozen yards farther along the river, but without result ; and on stepping onwards the river wound along a dell amongst the great beech trees, with the sunlight flashing from the surface and turning to bronzed silver patch after patch of bracken that spread its broad fronds in glistening sheets five and six feet high.

There was no tempting fishing-place here among the broad slopes, but beyond there was more than one favourite spot from which in times past the boy had taken many a speckled beauty, and to reach one of these he was pressing on with arms raised, and creel and rod held high, simply wading, as it were, through the rustling bracken, and every now and then beating back some frond that attacked his face, when, all at once, he stopped short, with his heart beating fast, for there was a quick rush, and something sprang up from almost at his feet and dashed away.

The bracken was so thick that all he saw was the quivering fronds, and, with no other thought than to catch a glimpse of the deer he had started from its lair, Waller rapidly gave a turn to the ferrule which made one rod of its two joints, and, using the butt to strike right and left at the ferns which impeded his way, he dashed on for about a dozen yards, and then stopped short. For he had brought his quarry to bay, forcing it to turn upon him fiercely, while the boy's heart beat faster still from the exertion mingled with his startled surprise.

But it was no fat buck with palmated antlers ready to be thrown forward for a fierce attack, for in his rapid glance amongst the bracken Waller found himself face to face with a lad of about his own age—no poaching gipsy, given to preying upon the indwellers of the forest, but a strange-looking, wild-eyed being, sunken of cheek, hollow of eye, and with long unkempt hair hanging about his shoulders.   Yet he was no threatening beggar, for, in spite of his garments being muddied, stained, and torn, he was well dressed, but menacing of aspect all the same ; for as he stood there, bareheaded and fierce, there was danger in his dark flashing eyes, and a gleam of white, as, like those of some animal, his thin lips were drawn from his glistening teeth.

" Who are you ?   What do you want ? " cried Waller, in his excitement ; while, as the words left his lips, there was a quick movement upon the stranger's part, and he felt for and drew something from his breast.

The next moment he was presenting a big flintlock pistol at his pursuer's head.

CHAPTER II.

A SURRENDER.

WALLER had a glimpse of the pistol as it was suddenly presented at his head, and then he only saw what seemed to be a round, rusty ring, through which he peered at nothing, but in full expectation of seeing a puff of smoke and hearing a report, while in the quick flash of thought that darted through his brain, the question he asked himself was, " Will it kill me ? "

But he did not stop to think, in this startling, novel position, for he acted simultaneously. As quick as his thought he gave a turn to the lower joint of his rod, separated the two pieces, and delivered a cut with the butt end, which took effect upon the presented weapon, knocking it out of its holder's hands, and then, tossing the rod aside, he sprang forward and closed, while the stranger, breathing hard, finding himself unarmed, tried to get a grip at his adversary's throat, failed, and wound his arms well round him instead, following this up by trying to lift Waller from the ground and throw him backward.

The next moment the beautiful little miniature tropic forest of ferns was faring badly, being kicked, broken, and trampled down as the two boys, breathing hard and panting with their exertions, swayed here and there, and wherever they planted foot there came up a curious crackling sound, for beneath the huge trees the earth was thickly covered with beechmast.

" Brute—savage ! "

Whop !

The dull sound was caused by the wild-looking young stranger coming down flat upon his back. For after a brief struggle, during the first part of which he was furious and strong, all his power seemed to depart at once like a blown-out flame, while Waller, who had grown stronger moment by moment, and hotter with temper as he wrestled here and there, put an end to the struggle as cleverly as any wrestler by heaving up the frantic youth, and falling with him to the earth.

For quite a minute they lay motionless, arms interlocked and chest to chest, their breath coming and going with a hoarse, harsh

sound, and their eyes glaring as they looked
defiance one at the other. Then, as the
conquered stranger's face grew more savage,
Waller's, in his triumph, slowly softened down
into a smile, and as he recovered his breath, he
said triumphantly :

" Done you, in spite of your old pistol !   I
say, was it loaded ? "

There was no reply, but the panting of the
stranger's breast seemed to grow louder.

" You coward ! " he groaned out, at last, in
a despairing tone.

" Ha, ha ! " laughed Waller.   " Brute,
savage, and now coward ! Why, you were
the coward to aim at me with a pistol when
I had nothing but a stick. Suppose it had
gone off ! "

" I wish it had," panted the prostrate boy,
with a vicious look.

" What !   Why, it might have killed me ! "
cried Waller.

"I wish it had," repeated the boy viciously.

" Stuff !   You are savage because you are
beaten."

" Get off ! " cried the stranger ; and he
made a desperate effort to throw his adversary from his chest, but only for Waller to
wrench out his hands, plant them upon the

other's breast, and thrust him down helpless and exhausted, while he raised himself up, got well astride, and sat up, laughing in the stranger's face, as he raised one hand and dragged the strap of the creel over his head and tossed it aside.

"Got rid of you," he muttered. "There, it's no good," he cried. "I have you quite tight. If you try to get up again I will give you such a drubbing."

"Oh—h!" groaned the boy addressed, passionately; and his breast heaved with the despairing, hysterical sobs that struggled for utterance.

"Ah, that's right!" cried Waller. "You had better lie still. I am too strong for a fellow like you."

"Yes," panted the other; "I'm beaten. It's all over now."

"Then you give in?" cried Waller, who grew more and more excited in his triumph, while he gazed down at the distorted countenance beneath him, wondering who the lad was and why there was a something un-English in his accent and the turn of his words, though they sounded native all the same.

"Yes, I give up," panted the boy; "and

you can be proud of having mastered a poor
starving wretch who never did you any
harm."

"No, because I stopped you," cried Waller.
"Who are you, and where did you steal that
pistol?"

"It was my own," said the other proudly.

"But what were you doing with that pistol
here?—poaching, I suppose? Lucky for you
my fine fellow, that I stopped you. Do you
know what would have happened to you if
you had killed one of the deer? Ha, ha, ha!
Killed one of the deer! Why, you could not
have hit a haystack with that thing."

"Deer!" cried the lad. "I did not want
to kill the deer."

"Don't believe you!" cried Waller.

The lad's face flushed, and an indignant
flash darted from his eyes.

"How dare you doubt my word of honour,"
he cried. "Here, let me get up."

"Shan't! Lie still!" shouted Waller, fling-
ing out his doubled fist and holding it within
a few inches of his prisoner's nose. "Your
word of honour, eh? Why, who do you call
yourself, my dirty, ragged Jack, with your
honour! Who are you, and where do you
come from?"

" Yes, you are a coward," said the lad bitterly, " or you would not insult a gentleman lying weak and helpless at your mercy."

Waller felt a little touched.

" Oh, I don't want to insult you," he said : " and perhaps I am as much of a gentleman as you are. But look here ; who are you ? "

" You know," said the lad bitterly. " I give up, I tell you. Be content that you have got the upper hand of me. I won't struggle against fate ; only make me one promise," he continued, in a bitter, mocking tone.

" Well, what is it ? " said Waller.

" Come and see your prisoner hung, for I suppose your brutal Dutchmen will not have me shot."

" I say," said Waller, staring more wonderingly than ever at his prisoner, " you are using very fine language. Are you a bit off your head ? Who wants to hang or shoot you ? What Dutchmen ? "

" The enemy—the brutal soldiery, of course."

" I say, look here, I don't know what you are talking about," said Waller, " and I don't know who you are, only that you jumped out at me like a highwayman with a pistol. I say, what are you ? "

" One of the spies, I suppose," said the
boy mockingly. " One of the poor unfor-
tunate wretches you people are hunting
through the woods."

" Nonsense ! " cried Waller. " You must
be fancying all this. There are no soldiers
here hunting people. Do you know where
you are ? "

" Yes ; in the New Forest."

" That's right, and in the part my father
holds the shooting over. But," continued
Waller, showing his white teeth, " he wouldn't
want to shoot you if he were at home ; you
are not fat enough. Pooh ! Nobody would
want to shoot a boy like you."

" Boy ! Who do you call a boy ? " cried
the poor fellow, flushing up again.

" Why, you, of course. You are no older
than I am, and I am a boy."

" Well, never mind that. You have made
me a prisoner. What are you going to do
next ? "

" Well, I think I am going to pick up that
pistol, wherever it lies."

" Bah ! " cried the prisoner. " I only did
it to scare you off. It isn't loaded."

" Oh ! " said Waller. " Well, that's one
to you. I couldn't tell."

" What are you going to do with me now ? "
said the lad haughtily. " Chain me ? "

" Chain you ! " said Waller, laughing,
" why, you are not a dog. I am not going to
do anything with you. I don't want you."

" No ; but you want the blood-money, I
suppose."

" There you go again," cried Waller pettishly. " Chains and blood ! I say, do you
know what you are talking about ? Blood-
money ? "

" Yes ; the reward for taking me."

" Reward ! For taking you ? "

" Yes, where are your bloodhounds ? "

" Well, you are a rum chap," said Waller,
laughing. " You talk like a fellow in a
romance. We have no bloodhounds. We
have a pointer, a water-spaniel, and a
retriever. Why, what sort of an idea have
you got in your head about bloodhounds
hunting you ? "

" I—I meant the soldiers," said the poor
fellow faintly : and his eyes began to close
" Let me sit up, please. I think I'm dying."

CHAPTER III.

THE words sounded so real, and there was such a deathly aspect in the pallor and the cold perspiration that started upon the prostrate lad's ghastly-looking face, that Waller was convinced at once, and quickly rising from where he sat he bent over and raised the lad's head a little, but only to lay it down again as the poor fellow fell back quite insensible.

But the attack passed off as quickly as it had come, and, relieved by the removal of the heavy pressure upon his chest, he began to breathe more freely, his eyes opened slowly in a wild stare of wonder as if he could not comprehend where he was, and then, as his senses fully returned, a faint smile dawned upon his thin lips.

"Don't laugh at me," he said. "It was like a great girl. I must have fainted dead away."

"Yes, you did, and no mistake," said Waller. "Come down to the stream and have a drink of water.—If I let you get up you won't try to escape?"

" No," said the lad bitterly, as he raised one hand, and let it fall again heavily amongst the bracken. " I am as weak as a child."

" Yes," said Waller, " you are. Now, look here ; you remember what you said about the honour of a gentleman ? "

The lad bowed his head slightly.

" You are a gentleman ? "

" Yes."

" Then give me your word that you won't try to escape."

" I will not try to escape. I could not if I wished. I tell you it is all over now, I am taken at last."

" I say," cried Waller, gazing at the poor fellow anxiously, " why are you here ? What have you done ? " And then slowly, and in almost a whisper, as he glanced sharply round for the pistol, " You haven't killed anybody, have you ? "

" Killed ! No ! What have I done ? Nothing that should disgrace a gentleman. Nothing but fight for the cause of my lawful king."

Waller looked at the lad curiously, for his words and the wildness of his looks again brought up the idea that he was a little off his head.

" But I say," he said, " if you were fighting,

as you call it, for your lawful king, why should the soldiers be after you ? "

" Because I am an enemy—a follower of the Stuarts."

" Oh," said Waller, in a puzzled tone, as the lad slowly and painfully rose, and then snatched at something to save himself, for he reeled. " Here, I say, you are weak," cried Waller, saving him from falling, " lean on me. The stream is just over there," and he led his feeble adversary down the slope to the nearest opening where he could lie down and reach over the bank to drink from the clear water in the most ancient and natural way—that is, by lowering his lips till they touched the surface.

The lad drank deeply, and then rose to a sitting position, making no effort to stand.

" Ah," he said faintly, " I feel better now. There," he went on, " I suppose you didn't know the soldiers were here ? "

Waller shook his head, content to listen.

" They are ; and you know all about the trouble—about the Stuarts making another stand for their rights ? "

" Oh, not much," said Waller. " I have read, of course, about the Old Pretender and the Young Pretender."

" Pretenders ! " said the lad bitterly.
" Those who fought for their rights as heirs
to the British Crown. They are at rest, but an
heir still lives, and it is his fortunes we follow."

" Oh," said Waller thoughtfully. " Yes,
I have heard of him—in France," and he
looked more curiously in the other's eyes as
he asked his next question, thinking the while
of the slight accent in the lad's speech.

" But you have not come from there ? "

" Yes," said the lad quietly, and with a
bitter tone of sadness in his words ; " we
crossed over from Cherbourg—oh, it must be
a month ago."

" We ? " said Waller inquiringly.

" Yes ; I came with my father and four
other gentlemen to Lymington."

" And are they here in the forest ? "

The lad looked at him wonderingly.

" No," he said ; " they were all hunted
down like wild beasts—treated as spies."

" And where are they now ? " said Waller
eagerly.

" Who knows ? " replied the lad sadly.
" Lingering in prison, if they have not already
been shot. Quick ! Tell me," he continued,
catching Waller by the arm. " My father !
Have you heard anything about him ? "

" I ?   No," said Waller.   " Oh, surely not
shot !   But in this quiet country place at the
Manor we hear so little of what is going on.
I can't help being so ignorant about all these
things."

" You are all the happier, perhaps," said
the lad sadly.

" Oh, I don't know," said Waller.   " I
am afraid I don't know much about what's
going on.   I am fond of being out here in the
woods.   It is holiday-time now my father's
out.   But I say," he continued, with a frank
laugh, " isn't it rather funny that you and I
should be talking together like this, after—
you know—such a little while ago ? "

" Yes, I suppose so ; but I thought you
were one of the enemy coming to take
me."

" Yes," said Waller ; " and I don't know
what I thought about you when I was looking
down the barrel of that pistol."

" I—I beg your pardon," faltered the lad.
" I was half mad."

" Quite mad, I think," said Waller to himself.   Then aloud, " But, I say, why were you
here ? "

" I was hiding ; trying to get down to the
coast and make my way back to France.   The

soldiers have been hunting me for days, but I have escaped so far."

" To get back to France ? " said Waller. " But are you not English ? "

" Yes, of course. Don't I speak like an Englishman ? "

" Well, there is a little something queer about it," said Waller—" a sort of accent."

" I said English," continued the other, " but my family, the Boynes, are of Irish descent, and staunch followers of the Stuarts."

" Yes ; but that's all over now, you know," said Waller. " Don't you think you had better give all that up and go back ? "

" I was trying to go back," said the lad despairingly.

" Or stop here."

" You talk like a follower of the Pretender," said the lad bitterly.

" That I don't ! " cried Waller indignantly. " My father is a magistrate, and a staunch supporter of King George. But there, I didn't mean to talk like that," he cried, as he noted the change that came over his companion's face. " Here, I say, never mind about politics. You look—well, very ill. Hadn't you better go home ? "

"Go home ! How ? Separated from my
friends, who perhaps by now are dead ! "
The words came with a sob, " Go ! How ?
Hunted from place to place like a wolf ! "
He tried to rise, but sank back. " Ill ?
Yes," he groaned ; " deadly faint. You don't
know what I have suffered. I am starving."

"How long have you been here ? "
said Waller, whose sympathies were growing
more and more strong in favour of his
prisoner.

" I don't know. Days."

" But why were you starving ? " said
Waller half-indignantly.

" Why should I not be ? " said the boy
bitterly. " Alone in these wilds."

" Well," cried Waller. " I shouldn't have
starved if I had been like you. I should have
liked it, and had rather a jolly time," and he
gazed hard at the delicate-looking lad, whose
very aspect, in spite of his disorder, suggested
that he had led a gentle life, possibly mingling
with the followers of the Court.

The gaze was returned—a gaze full of
wonderment.

" What would you have done ? " said the
stranger. " Eaten the bitter acorns and the
leaves ? "

" No," cried Waller, laughing, " I should just think not ! Why, I should have done as Bunny Wrigg would—scraped myself out a good hole in the side of one of the sandpits, half-filled it with dry bracken for my bed, made a corner for my fire somewhere outside, and then had a good go in at the rabbits and the fish ; and there are plenty of pig-nuts and truffles, if you know how to hunt for them. There are several places where you can get mushrooms out in the open part among the furze where the grass grows short ; and then there's that kind that grows on the oak trees. You can trap birds, too, or knock over ducks that come down the stream if you are lucky. I have several times got one with a bow and arrow. Oh, there are lots of ways to keep from starving out in the woods."

" Ah," said the lad feebly, " you are a country boy. I come from French cities, and know nothing of these things."

" Oh ! " said Waller thoughtfully. " What have you had to eat this morning ? "

The boy laughed sadly.

" I have picked some leaves," he said.

" Picked some leaves ! " cried Waller contemptuously. " Why didn't you hunt for some of the hens' eggs ? There are lots about here, half-wild, that have strayed away from the farms and taken to the woods. 'Of course a raw egg is not so good as one nicely cooked, but it would keep a fellow from looking as bad as you do. Here, I say, I am sorry that I knocked you about so. I didn't know that you were so bad as this."

" It doesn't matter now," was the reply. " You had better give me up to the soldiers at once. I suppose they will give me something to eat. My pride's all gone now, and I only want to get it over and bring it to an end. It's very contemptible, I know, but it is very horrible, all the same."

" What is ? " said Waller quickly.

" To feel that you are starving to death."

" There, now you are talking nonsense," said Waller warmly. " Why, of course it is. Who's going to starve to death ? Here, I suppose I oughtn't to help you ? "

" No ; I am an enemy. Give me up to the soldiers as quickly as you can."

" Bother the soldiers ! " cried Waller hotly. " Let them do their work themselves. I don't know anything about enemies. You are half-starved and ill, and if you stop till I come back I'll run off and get you something to eat. I could take you home with me at once, but if I did the servants would see you, and begin to talk, and then it might get to the ears of the soldiers, if there are any about. Don't run away till I come back with them," continued Waller, with a mocking laugh. " You don't want any more water, do you ? "

The lad shook his head.

" Then creep in there under those ferns. Nobody could see you even if he came by, and Bunny Wrigg is the only one likely to be about here. Clever as he is, I don't suppose he would spy you out. Why, I shouldn't have seen you if you hadn't started up as you did— That's right. I shan't be long."

Waller snatched up the two joints of his rod, and the creel which he had thrown down, and started off at a smart trot in and out amongst the great beeches, not traversing the way by which he had come, but striking a bee-line for home.

CHAPTER IV.

A RAID ON THE LARDER.

BRACKENDENE was the very model of an Elizabethan country house, with clusters of twisted chimneys, and ivy clinging to the red bricks everywhere that it could find a hold.

There was an attractive porch opening out upon the well-kept pleasaunce, but, instead of going straight to it, Waller looked sharply to right and left, saw nobody and heard nothing but a dull, distant *thump, thump,* and the barking of a dog from somewhere at the back.

The next minute he was through one of the dining-room casements, and crossed into the hall, where he stood listening for a moment or two to the *thump, thump,* which now sounded nearer.

" That's Martha at her churn," he muttered. " How stupid it seems ! Anyone would think I was a thief."

He felt like one as he crossed the hall, opened a big oak door cautiously, and made his way into the great red-brick-floored kitchen, where from an opening to his left the thumping of the churn came louder still, accompanied by a dull humming sound, something like the buzz of a musical bee, but which was intended by the utterer to represent a tune.

Waller nodded his head with satisfaction, and went off to his right out of the kitchen into a cool stone passage, and then through a door into a stone-floored larder, whose wire-covered, ivy-shaded windows gave upon the north.

But Waller Froy had no thought for the situation of the larder. His attention was taken up by about three-quarters of a raised pork-pie, which he took off the dish, and, after a moment's hesitation, drew his big trout out of the creel and dabbed it in where the pie had stood, making the latter take the fish's place in the creel.

" Make it taste a bit," muttered the boy. " Can't stop to find a cloth, and he will be too hungry to notice. Now for some bread."

The larder was not his place, but the boy was quite at home there, due to surreptitious visits connected with fishing excursions and provisions for lunch.

Taking the great brown lid off a bread-pan, he placed it on the floor and pounced upon a loaf, which he broke in two and crammed into his fishing-creel. He then rose up and looked round, till his eyes lighted upon a big jug full of creamy-looking milk, which he annexed at once, and then made for the door, passed through the kitchen, where the thumping and musical buzz still went on, made his way back to the dining-room, and through the window again out into the garden, and then passed breathlessly into the dense forest once again, panting slightly from his exertions.

" I have as good a right to the things as anybody," he muttered, to quiet his uneasy conscience, " and if Martha asks me if I took the pie I shall say yes, of course. I am not going to enter into explanations. Let her think I was hungry and wanted some lunch ; and if she does think it's my doing—oh ! " he ejaculated, " she will know it was when she finds the fish ; and there—if I didn't leave the great cover of the pan on the floor ! Bother ! " he ejaculated. " I am master when father's out, and I shall do as I like. Wish I could," he grumbled, as he hurried along, not so fast as he wished, for his way was rough and tangled, and the jug of milk was very full, besides being an awkward thing to carry steadily where brambles continually crossed the path and the thorny strands of the dog-rose hung down from on high as if fishing for everyone who passed. " I should like to think about what to do," mused Waller to himself, " but it only makes one so uncomfortable. This fellow must be one of the King's enemies, and if I am helping the King's enemies, shan't I be committing high treason ? Oh, bother ! " he cried aloud. " I am going to give a poor fellow who is starving something to eat, and, enemy or no, I am sure if King George saw him starving he'd do the same. There, I won't think about it any more."

He reached the spot where he had left his new acquaintance, in a state of repentance because he had not lowered the milk by taking a good draught, the consequence being that he had spilt a good deal.

All was perfectly still, and he began to wade through the ferns, and then stopped to look straight before him, and then sharply to right and left.

" Why, he isn't a gentleman, after all," muttered the boy. " He's gone. It was just in there that I told him to crawl, and—— no, it was farther on, by that next beech— no——oh, I say, how much alike all these places are ! I believe I must have passed it."

He stood still and whistled. There was no reply. Then he whistled again, and, after glancing about him, hazarded a call.

" Hi ! Hullo ! Where are you ?—It's all right ; no soldiers near."

There was a faint rustling then amongst the bracken, and the strangers head was slowly raised some thirty yards away.

Waller hurried to him.

" What made you change your place ? " he said, as he came up.

" Change my place ? I have not moved."

" Never mind. There, sit down now. Here's something to take off the hunger. There, if I didn't forget a knife ! Never mind ; mine will do. It's quite clean. That's right. No-body's likely to come by here. Take a good drink of this first."

He placed the jug in the lad's hand as he seated himself between the great buttress-like roots of a huge beech : and after that long, deep drink there was an interval of time during which Waller watched, with a feel-ing of wonder, the ravenous manner in which his new friend—or enemy—partook of food.

" I am ashamed," he muttered ; " I am ashamed. But eat some, too."

" Oh, no ; go on," said Waller.

" I can't eat another mouthful unless you join."

" Oh, very well ; there is plenty," said Waller, " and seeing you eat has made me hungry, too."

No more words were spoken for a time, and at last, with the hunger of both pretty well assuaged, Waller began to note the humour of the position, and in a half-bantering way exclaimed :

" Here, I say, you ought to leave a snack for the soldiers when they come."

The lad's hand dropped, and he turned, with a wild look, to fix his eyes on Waller's.

" Ah," he said, the next moment, with his face softening, " you are laughing at me."

" Well, suppose I am. It's because I am pleased to see you better now."

" Better ! Yes. I think you have saved my life," said the lad softly. " I say, I wish we could be friends—but no ; impossible. You could not be, with one like me."

" I don't see why not," said Waller. " We are good enough friends now. There, I am sorry I knocked you about so much and

treated you as I did.   I didn't know you were
so weak and hungry. Will you shake hands ? "

" Will I shake hands ? " cried the lad, with
all the effusion of a young Frenchman, and
catching the one which Waller stretched out,
he held it tightly for a few moments between
his own, holding it until Waller drew it away.

" There," he said, " I must be going back
now.   There isn't much left, but I must
have the empty basket. You had better lie
down here and have a good rest, and I will
come back to you in the evening and see if I
can't think out some way of helping you to
get down to Lymington."

" To Lymington ?   Yes ! " cried the boy
eagerly ;   for now that he was somewhat
refreshed the light seemed to come back into
his eyes, and a certain eagerness into his whole
aspect.   " But, look here," he said, " a little
while ago I thought I had nothing to do but
lie down and die ; now you have made me
feel as if I want to live.   Could you—can you
find out whether there are any soldiers
near ? "

" I don't know, but I'll try," said Waller.
" But I say, talk about soldiers—we never
picked up that pistol, and I don't believe we
could find it now."

" Here it is," said the lad, pointing to his breast. " I crawled about till I found it after you had gone."

" Then you had better give it to me to put away. Pistols are nasty things."

Waller held out his hand, but the lad shrank back, with a suspicious look.

" Oh, very well," said Waller, rising ; " don't trust me unless you like."

" I do trust you," cried the lad eagerly ; and, snatching out the pistol, he pressed it into the other's hand.

" There, they will be wondering what has become of me," cried Waller. " I will come back and see you in the evening, and by then I shall have thought of somewhere for you to hide to-night. Good-bye."

Waller hurried off, thinking deeply to himself, and making the best of his way for about a hundred yards.

" I wish I hadn't brought away his pistol," he said. " He will be thinking again that I am going to betray him. Here, I shall take it back."

He made his way as fast as he could to where he had left his new friend, expecting to see him raise his head as he drew dear ; but he looked in vain, for when he reached the spot, and parted the tall bracken, he was unable to find him for a few minutes, and when he did, the figure was recumbent, utterly exhausted, and sleeping hard, while he did not even move as Waller bent over him and carefully thrust the pistol into his breast.

CHAPTER V.

DUTY OR MERCY.

" Oh, here you are, Master Waller ! " said
Bella, as he marched into the house.
" Where have you been ? "

" Fishing," said Waller abruptly.

" But why didn't you come back to your
dinner ? "

" Because I have been out in the forest,
and—fishing, I tell you. Why ? "

" Because Martha has been in such a way,
There was your dinner kept three hours, till
it was quite spoiled, and then we said it was
no use to keep it any longer ; and Martha is
in a way."

" What about ? " said Waller absently, for
his thoughts were still in the forest along with
the young stranger.

" Because she says she won't put up with it,
and if you are to go in and out of the pantry
helping yourself to what you please, she will
complain to master as soon as he comes
back."

" Oh, very well, Bella," giving the fresh-
looking servant girl a nod.

" But aren't you hungry ? "

" No."

" Well, you are a boy ! You will want something to eat with your tea, won't you ? "

" Yes, I suppose so. But I say, Bella, have you heard anything about there being soldiers in the forest ? "

" Oh, yes," said the girl eagerly. " You haven't seen any of them, have you ? "

" I ? No," said Waller quickly. " What have you heard ? "

" Oh, I only heard what Tony Gusset said to Martha when he came in to talk to her last night."

" What ! " cried Waller. " Was that old stupid here last night ? "

" Yes ; but he wasn't here long. Martha won't let him stay. She soon bundles him off again. She told me that he wouldn't be so fond of his sister if she wasn't the cook and couldn't ask him to have something to eat when he came. She does hate to see him here."

" But what did he tell her ? "

" Oh, I don't know," said the girl pettishly.

" Yes, you do, Bella. Tell me."

" Well, will you promise to be a good boy and come back to your meals at proper times, and not keep everything waiting about ? "

" Oh, yes, of course. Now what was it ? "

" Oh, he told her that the French had landed on the coast to turn the King off the throne and put a new foreign one on it, and that the soldiers had met them and beaten them, all but a few who were spies, and had hidden themselves in the forest ; but they were catching them all till there were hardly any left, and they were looking for them. And Tony Gusset said there was a reward of a hundred pounds offered for every one that was caught, and he meant to catch one and make himself rich."

" He had better mind his mending shoes and hammering his old lapstone," cried Waller, with an unwonted show of anger. " What's it got to do with him ? "

" There, now, if that isn't funny ! " said the girl, clapping her hands. " Why, that's just what Martha said to him, and he quite quarrelled with her. He said it was his duty as the village constable to apprehend all vagabonds, and that if his sister did not know how to pay him more respect he should not stoop to come and speak to her again."

" Well done, cook ! " cried Waller, laughing. " What then ? "

" Why, she up and told him that he was only a lazy vagabond himself, for he never did hardly any work, and that since he had been made constable the place had not been big enough to hold him. But there, I can't stop talking here ; I have got to get your tea. What am I to say to Martha about your taking that pork-pie ? "

" Nothing," said Waller gruffly.

" But she meant it for your tea."

" Well, I had it for lunch instead. Now go away and don't bother."

" Well, I am sure ! " cried the girl. " What's come to you, Master Waller ? You're as cross as two sticks."

" Of course I am, if you stop chattering here instead of getting me my tea."

" But it won't be tea-time for another hour."

" I tell you it's always tea-time for anyone who hasn't had any dinner, so go and get it at once."

Bella went out of the room, and gave the door a regular whisk to make it bang, but repented directly after, and let it strike against her foot, so that it was closed quietly.

Waller jumped up from his chair in an unwonted state of excitement, as soon as he was alone, and began to walk hurriedly up and down the room.

" Then it's all true," he mused. " There are soldiers about, and if they catch that poor fellow they will march him off to prison— and he is so ill after being hunted about. Oh, it's too bad ! " he continued, growing more and more excited. " And there's no knowing what they would do. Why, they hung the poor wretch who wasn't much more than a boy for stealing that sheep ; and I believe it was only because he was hungry and out of work. Here, I know I oughtn't to interfere, but father isn't at home, and I feel as if I ought to do something. I want to do something. It seems so horrid. Suppose it had been I who went on like that poor fellow did. I don't think I should ever do such a thing as he has, but what did he say ? He came over with his father. Well, suppose I went over to France with my father. Of course, it isn't likely, but one might have done such a thing, and I daresay they have got a New Forest in France. To be sure they have, and I know its name—Fountainebleau. Only fancy if I were being hunted through that place by soldiers. Ugh ! If there was a young fellow there found me—a young fellow

just about my age—and did not help me, he'd
be a brute."

In his excitement the boy went on marching
up and down the quaint, old panelled dining-
room, with his fists clenched and his eyes
staring, as he recalled the scene in the woods
that morning.

Just as he was opposite the door it was
thrown open quickly by Bella, who entered
with the tea-tray, and who stopped short,
startled by the boy's fierce looks, while as
he turned sharply round to march to the other
end of the room, Bella hurriedly placed the
tea-tray upon the table, and then hastened
back to go and tell Martha the cook that she
believed Master Waller was going mad.

CHAPTER VI.

A GOOD APPETITE.

" Yes, I'll mad him," retorted the cook, " if he comes meddling with my larder when my back's turned. I have a very great mind not to finish cooking those sausage-meat cakes for his tea—behaving like that when the Squire's out ! "

But all the same Martha Gusset, who was a pleasant, portly dame, went back to her fire to continue her hurried cooking for her young master's evening meal.

Meanwhile, without a thought of eating or drinking, Waller was still marching up and down the dining-room making up his mind what he should do ; and, this made up, he waited impatiently for the maid's return to finish her preparations, which were concluded by her bearing in a covered dish which evidently contained something hot and steaming, the vapour which escaped from beneath the cover having a very pleasant, savoury odour.

" There, Master Waller," said the girl good-humouredly. " Now, do make a good tea, there's a good boy, and you know what cook is ; she don't like to be put out. I know what I should do if I was you."

" What ? " said Waller, rather surlily.

" Go into the kitchen as soon as you have done tea, and tell her that you never had anything nicer than those cakes ; and she will be so pleased that she won't say another word about the pie."

" Oh, very well," said Waller, who was making another plan.

" That's a good boy. Between you and me, Master Waller, Martha's as nice as nice, but she's just as proud and stuck up about her cooking as her brother is about being con- stable. Ring when you have done, please."

Waller nodded, and lifted up the dish- cover, which the girl took from his hand, and then, nodding pleasantly, hurried out of the room.

The boy's actions the next minute were rather curious, for he followed to the door, turned the little handle that shot the small bolt into its socket, and then, after a con- spirator-like glance at both the windows, he went to the bookcase and took down six or eight books from the lower shelf, to place them on a chair, before he hurried back to the table, caught up a nice hot plate and a fork, and then transferred half a dozen out of the eight nicely browned meat buns from the dish, carried the plate to the opening in the book-shelf, and pushed it as far back as it would go.

Returning to the table, he paid his next attentions to a little pile of hot and buttered bread cakes, a kind of food in which Martha excelled. Taking up a couple of these, one in each hand, he was moving once more to-wards the bookcase, but turned back directly.

" Sure to be dusty in there," he muttered ; and, turning back to the table, he deposited the cakes in a plate, which the next minute was standing beside its fellow in the back of the bookcase.

The boy's next act was to replace the books ; but there was not room for them and the plates, and the consequence was that they projected about a couple of inches from the edge of the shelf, while when he tried to shut the glass bookcase door, it too, stood a little way out.

" Don't suppose she will see," he muttered, and, satisfied now with what he had done, he went and unbolted the dining-room door, and, feeling very guilty, took his place at the table, poured out his tea, was very liberal with the sugar and milk, and then helped himself to one of the two sausage cakes left and a slice of hot bread.

He had got about half-way through Martha's appetising cake and had taken three good half-moon bites out of a slice of hot bread, thinking deeply the while, and munching mechanically with his mouth full, but quite unconscious of the flavour of that which he ate, when the door was thrown open and Bella entered, making the boy jump and feel more guilty than ever.

" It's only me, Master Waller. I have just come to see how you are getting on," continued the girl, as she advanced towards the table, scanning everything that it held, " and whether I can—oh, my ! " she burst out, snatching up her apron and holding it to her mouth to try and stifle back an immoderate burst of laughter.

The next moment she had rushed out of the room, this time allowing the door to bang behind her, while Waller jumped up, staring hard at the partly closed bookcase door as if to read there the cause of the girl's quick exit.

" She must have been watching at the key-hole," he muttered to himself, for a guilty conscience needs no accuser, " and she's gone to tell cook."

But it was something quite different that Bella was telling her fellow-servant, after throwing herself down in one of the kitchen chairs and laughing hysterically till she cried and choked.

" Oh, don't be such a stupid," grunted plump Martha, standing over her and thumping her back. " What is it you have seen ? Don't keep it all to yourself. What 'are you laughing at ? You will have a fit directly."

" Oh ! oh ! oh—h—h ! " sobbed Bella. " Do leave off, cook. You *hurt.*"

" Then tell me what you are laughing at."

" He's—he's—he's—oh, dear !—oh, dear ! I never saw such a sight in my life ! I hadn't been gone more than five minutes when—ho ! ho ! ho ! ho ! "

" Look here," cried cook, who was enjoying her fellow- servant's mirth, and who began thumping again at poor Bella's back, " do you want me to thump it out of you ? "

" Oh, no, no, no, no, no ! Do a-done, cook ! " sobbed out Bella, hysterically and incoherently. " Not more than five minutes, and his mouth so full he couldn't speak, and his eyes staring at me out of his head, and he had gobbled up nearly all the sausage cakes and all the hot bread, and I don't know how many cups of tea he had had, but the one before him was quite full. But oh, Martha, do a-done, and let me laugh it out, or I shall die ! "

Plump Martha's face was wreathed with smiles, and she chuckled a little audibly at her fellow-servant's mirth, while her pleasant little vanity was agreeably tickled at the appreciation of her culinary efforts all the while.

" You are such a stupid, Bella," she said, good-humouredly. " When once you begin to laugh you never know how to leave off. I don't see anything to laugh at. Poor dear boy, he'd had no dinner, and only a morsel of cold pork pie since breakfast, and he does like my cakes."

CHAPTER VII.

SECRET PREPARATIONS.

WALLER'S appetite was gone. The girl seemed to have taken it out of the room with her, and the boy thrust his hands into his pockets and sat thinking for some time about his plans, and ended by rising from his hardly touched meal to cross to the bell. But a fresh idea occurred to him, and, going back to the table, he took his untouched cup, carried it carefully to the open window, and emptied it upon a flower-bed ; then, returning the cup, he rang the bell, waited till he heard Bella's step in the hall, and then began to parade in a sort of " sentry go " up and down in front of the partly open bookcase, while the maid, after a glance at the boy's averted countenance and frowning face, not daring to catch his eye for fear of bursting out into a fresh fit of laughter, began to clear the table.

Neither spoke till the task was pretty well finished, and then the girl looked up at Waller, next at the table, and lastly about the room.

" Well," she exclaimed, " if I couldn't declare that I brought two more plates ! "

Waller paid no apparent heed to the remark, but continued his " sentry go," breathing rather hard the while, till Bella left the room, when he uttered a low sigh of relief.

But the boy's thoughts had not been idle during this time, and as soon as he was free to carry out his plans he opened the door, listened to the murmur of voices in the kitchen, and then ran to the bookcase, took out his supply of provender, had another listen, and then ran with the two plates up-stairs, past the main set of bedrooms, and then up the next flight to a room in the front which was devoted to his pursuits.

Here he had books, tools, stuffed birds, fishing-tackle, a wonderfully untidy lot of specimen birds' nests and their eggs arranged on shelves ; in short, in addition to a pallet bedstead and bed that were very rarely used, a most glorious muddle of the odds and ends and collections dear to the heart of a country lad, all of which were under an interdict not to be touched by the brush, broom, or duster of the maids.

Waller's actions gave the key to his thoughts.

The cereal and carnal cakes were thrust into

a closet, and the boy proceeded then to turn down and feel the bed, over which he frowned and seemed in doubt ; but the next minute he had rushed out of the room and downstairs to his own chamber, to strip a couple of blankets from the bed, smooth it over again, and make it rougher than it was before, a fact which he grasped and puzzled over for a moment, before exclaiming, " Bother ! " and, after listening at the head of the stairs, he rushed up into his work-room with the blankets.

That seemed to him to be all that he could do, till it occurred to him that the room felt hot and stuffy, so he threw open the window, fastening back the casement, and stood gazing out at a great rugged old Scotch fir not many feet away, one apparently of great age, and which cut off a part of the view over the undulating greenery of the forest.

Quite satisfied now, and with a sigh of relief, the boy went out to the landing, carefully locked the door and pocketed the key.

" Let 'em think," he muttered with a grim smile upon his lips, " it's a curiosity I found in the woods."

By this time he was down in the gallery and passing his own chamber, where he stopped short, bringing himself up with the ejaculation—

"Oh! Bella will be at me about the blankets.! Bother! What shall I say? Tell her to mind her own business," he cried half-savagely; and as if to get away from his thoughts he ran down into the hall, snatched his cap from the stand, and then hurried away for the woods.

But it was not in his ordinary free and careless fashion, for his thoughts haunted him, and every now and then he kept turning round as if fancying that he was followed. Now his eyes were directed back at the old ivy-covered house, where he expected to see the maid watching him from one of the windows. Soon after, when the Manor was hidden by the clustering oaks that were scattered park-like among the fields, he was looking over his left shoulder to see if that was the fat village constable in the distance bending down so as to creep along unobserved, and not one of his father's mouse-coloured cows.

Hurrying on, and right into the forest, his next fancy was that he heard a distant shout, one that was answered, though it might have been an echo, and his heart beat a little faster as he set both sounds down to soldiers searching among the trees and hallooing to one another so as to keep in touch.

" Oh, I say," he muttered to himself, as he proceeded, keeping to the densest portions of the forest, and doubling the labour in threading his way, " who could have thought that it would make one feel so queer ? I haven't done anything—at least, nothing much—to mind, and here am I feeling as if I had been guilty of nobody knows what. No wonder that poor chap felt so bad and pulled out the pistol. What did he say his name was ? Boyne ? Let's see—Battle of the Boyne—where was that ? Oh, I know— King James, and he was a Stuart. Nonsense ! That couldn't have had anything to do with his name. Let's see ; I had better wait till it gets dusk, and then—oh, I'll risk it. I'll smuggle him up to the house and upstairs. But what about Joe Hanson ? Mustn' run against him. He's always pottering about outside the house towards evening, just as if he thought I wanted to go down the garden and help myself to apples and pears. Like his impudence, with his ' my garden ' and ' my fruit,' and all the rest of it ; and father said that I was to take what I liked, and that he should be proud to leave it to my discretion. It will come to a row one of these days, for I shall hit out at Master Joe, and

then he will go and complain. Bother Joe
Hanson ! I want to think about that poor
chap lying out there amongst the bracken.
What a miserable, haggard scarecrow he did
look, just like some poor beggarly tramp. But
one could feel that he was a gentleman as
soon as he began to speak. There ; best way
will be to take him boldly up to the front door
and right up the stairs, and chance it. One
never tries to play the sneak and get anywhere unseen without running bang up against
somebody."

These and similar thoughts so took up the
boy's attention that it was like a surprise to
him when, close upon sunset, and when the
shadows were deepening in the forest, he
found himself close to the spot where he had
left the fugitive ; and there he stopped short,
listening and then, feeling that he must not
seem to be peering about, he took out his
knife, cut down a nice straight rod of hazel,
and began to whittle and trim it, apparently
intent upon his task, but with his ears twitching and his lowered eyes peering to right and
left in every direction, as he seemed to be
unconsciously changing his position.

" Wish I were as clever as Bunny Wrigg,"
he muttered. " He's just like a fox for hiding,

throwing anyone off the scent. He'd have got here without anybody seeing him, while, for aught I know, I may have been watched all the time—by soldiers, perhaps. That must have been some of them I heard shouting. Oh, it is so queer," he muttered passionately, as he hacked off the twigs of the stout sapling. " Only this morning I was as happy as I could be, and now my head's all of a buzz with worry. . Wish I'd gone and found Bunny Wrigg and told him all ; he'd have helped me and enjoyed the job. I don't know, though. There's that hundred pounds reward. I am glad, after all, I didn't trust him. This is one of the things like father talked to me about where one has no business to trust anybody but oneself. Here, I mustn't go straight up to the hiding-place, in case I am watched. Oh, how suspicious I do feel ! "

Turning short round, he began to retrace his steps, acting as if he had fulfilled his purpose and come expressly for that hazel-rod, which he went on trimming, humming a tune the while, which unconsciously merged into one of the Scottish ditties about " Charley over the water."

He sauntered on for some distance, till, coming to what he considered a suitable spot, he glanced furtively to right and left without turning his head, and then, having pretty well trimmed his rod, he began to treat it as if it were a javelin, darting it right away before him, and running after it to catch it up and aim it with a good throw at a tree some yards away. He went through this performance four or five times over before aiming for a dense clump of the abundant bracken, into the midst of which he darted his mock spear, dashed in after it, and did not appear again, for the hazel-rod was left where it fell, and the boy was crawling rapidly on hands and knees beneath the great bracken fronds, keeping well out of sight till, judging by the towering beeches which he took for his bearings, he stopped at last, hot and panting with his exertions, close to where he had left the young spy.

CHAPTER VIII.

HELPING THE FUGITIVE.

WALLER had managed so well that he had only a few yards to go ; in fact, if the task had been undertaken by the tall gipsy-like woodland dweller, to whom he had referred as Bunny— a nickname, by the way, bestowed upon him by the boy from his rabbit-like habits, though they were more foxy, as Waller felt, but he liked him too well to brand him with such a name—it could not have been done better.

The next minute, with a vivid recollection of the pistol which had been thrust into the fugitive's breast, the boy was creeping forward and listening, till, as he came nearer, he became aware of a deep stertorous breathing, almost a snore, and, closing up, he bent over, to lay one hand on the hidden pistol, so as to be well on his defence, while with the other he gently shook the deep sleeper.

Waller expected that the poor fellow would start up in wild affright, but his touch only resulted in a dull, incoherent muttering, and the shake had to be repeated two or three times before the fugitive slowly sat up and gazed at him vacantly, laying one hand upon his burning forehead the while.

" Yes," he said slowly, " What is it ? "

" I have come back," said Waller. " Don't you know me ?   Why, you are not half awake yet.   It will be dark soon, quite dark by the time we get home, and I am going to take you there."

The poor fellow passed his hand two or three times across his forehead, as if to clear away some mist that hindered his perceptions.

"I say, you have had a splendid sleep," continued Waller.   " Feel better now ? "

" Sleep ?   Better ?   I don't know—don't know.   Yes, I do.   You came and brought me something to eat, and I have been to sleep and dreaming about—Oh ! " he groaned, and, leaning forward and covering his face with his hands, he began to rock himself to and fro as if the mental agony from which he suffered was too hard to bear.

Waller looked on in silence for a few moments, before reaching forward and laying his hand upon the poor fellow's shoulder, when the touch acted like magic.   His hands were caught in those of the fugitive, who rose painfully to his feet and spoke in a low, quick, hurried way.

" Yes," he said, " I am ready. Take me where you said ; but," he added, glancing sharply round with a wild and fevered look in his eyes, " did the soldiers come, or did I dream it ? "

" Dreamt it," said Waller emphatically.

" Ah ! " was sighed. " Am I speaking properly ? I—I don't quite know what I say. It's my head, I suppose—my head."

" You are not quite awake," said Waller encouragingly. " There, come down to the river and bathe your face. It's getting beautifully cool now ; and then we will go gently home through the woods."

The poor fellow nodded quickly, obeying his companion to the letter, and seeming to trust himself entirely in his hands,

He seemed a little clearer after lying down and bathing his face ; but as they walked slowly towards the Manor there were moments when he began to turn dizzy and reeled. But they reached the old Elizabethan house at last, quite in the dusk of evening, and, following out his settled plans, Waller led his companion in through the porch, across the hall, and upstairs, quite unseen, and rather breathless himself, while his companion seemed to have grown calmer. He unlocked the door of his den, threw it open, and closed it upon them with a sigh of relief, as he said,

"There, sit down in that old chair—gently, for the bottom's broken. This is my own room." Then, as the poor fellow sank back heavily in the very ancient chair, one that Waller had rescued from the lumber-room for his own particular use, he said, "I say: I won't be above a minute. Don't you stir. I am going downstairs to get a light."

There was no reply, and, hurriedly descending, Waller fetched candle and stick, to return and find the "something" that he had brought in from the forest fast asleep once more.

"Now we shall be all right," he said. "I have got some supper for you. What, asleep again?" he continued, more gently. "Well, you had better lie down. Here, I say, have a nap on the bed. Get up, and I'll help you. You had better undress."

The poor fellow grasped a portion of his wishes, and rose mechanically, reeled to the bed, and fell across it with his legs trailing upon the floor ; but a few minutes after, with his young host's help, he was properly installed outside, dressed as he was, to sink at once into a deep, feverish sleep.

There was no suppering that night for the stranger, who slept on, muttering quickly at intervals, and was still sleeping when Waller stole up to his side again and again at intervals during what seemed to be an interminably long night ; for though he pretended to go to bed, the boy could not sleep for more than an hour at a time, and when he did it was only to start up from some troubled dream connected with the incidents of the past day, for he was suffering badly from a new complaint—fugitive on the brain.

CHAPTER IX

IN HIDING.

" WHAT'S he doing now ? " said Martha. " Isn't going to be ill, is he ? "

" Ill ! " said Bella, contemptuously. " Not he ! "

" But he's shut up in that attic, isn't he ? "

" Yes, I told you so. Got another of those whim-whams in his head, and making a litter of some kind—skinning snakes or something that he's caught in the woods."

" Ugh ! " ejaculated cook. " If there's anything I can't abear it's them nasty scrawmy things. Did you tell him his dinner was ready ? "

" Yes, and he nearly snapped my head off."

" What does he want to be skinning snakes for ? " said the cook.

" Oh, I don't know—horrid things ! He's got about half a dozen up there as he did last year ; peels all the skins off, same as you do with the eels, and then turns them inside out again, fills them full of sand, and then twists them up and leaves them to dry."

" And what then ? " said cook.

" Pours all the sand out again."

" But, I say, has he got them up there alive before he skins them ? "

" I don't know as he has got any at all," said Bella shortly.

" Then why did you say he had ? "

" I didn't. I only said I supposed he had, because he's always skinning something or another. He's got owls, and stoats, and all sorts of things that he gets in the forest, or that nasty fellow Bunny Wrigg brings for him."

" Oh ! " said the cook. " Because I am not going to sleep upstairs if he's got live snakes to come crawling out of his room at all times in the night."

But though guilty of many such acts as the maid charged him with, Waller was not engaged with any taxidermic preparations, for his time during the past two days had been taken up in attendance upon the young fugitive.

For the first day the latter ate nothing, but passed the full twenty-four hours in a feverish sleep. Then he seemed to throw off the fever, and, thanks to his host, who was eager to supply him, gradually transformed himself from the miserable, ragged, famished object into such a specimen of humanity as made Waller smile with satisfaction.

" Why," he said, " if the soldiers did come they wouldn't know you again."

" Again ? " replied the lad. " They've never seen me."

" Well, I mean they wouldn't take you for a—for a——"

" There, say it," cried the lad sadly, " For a spy."

" I didn't mean spy," said Waller. " I meant fugitive."

" But they would. If I were questioned, what account could I give of myself ? I have tried to do the work for which I came—for which we came—and I have failed. I am not going to tell a lie."

" No, of course not," said Waller hotly ; " but you might hold your tongue, or tell any impudent beggar who dared to ask you questions, to mind his own business, if he didn't want to be kicked."

" Should you speak to the soldiers like that ? " said Boyne, with a smile.

" Of course," cried Waller. " What do I care for the soldiers ? "

" Ah ! " sighed the lad. " But never mind that. I am so grateful to you for all you have done."

" Oh, nonsense ! " cried Waller, flushing.

" People are always hospitable in the country."

" So I have heard," said the other ; " but,
if I had been your own brother you could not
have done more for me. You have saved my
life."

" Oh, nonsense ! I tell you. You make too
much of it. I never had a brother, but fellows
whom I have known at Winchester who have
—they are not so very fond of doing things for
one another. They generally like fighting and
knocking one another about. I suppose they
oughtn't to, but they quarrel more with their
brothers than they do with anyone else. But
you mustn't touch their brothers, for if you
do—oh my ! You have them on to you at
once. Here, I say, I wish you wouldn't talk
like that."

" Well, I will not. I don't want to go away
and leave you, but I must. I can think of
nothing else."

" But why ? "

" Because I am shut up here alone so much,
a prisoner."

" Yes, but it's only until it's safe for you to
go away. You must see that you ought to
be patient. There, I'll bring you up books
to read, to amuse you."

" I can't read them.   They wouldn't amuse
me with my mind in this state."

" Well, then, have a look at some of my
things," cried Waller, pulling out the drawer
of a big press.   " These are all traps and
springs with which I catch birds and animals
in the forest.   Bunny Wrigg taught me how
to make them and how to use them.   I wish
you knew him.   He's a capital fellow, and
knows the forest ten times better than I do."

" Oh, I don't want to know the forest—nor
your friend," said the lad wearily.   " I want
to be free to come and go—as free as the birds
and those little animals, the squirrels, that I
see out of the window."

" Yes, of course you do, and so you shall be
soon," cried Waller.   " But you haven't quite
recovered yet from that feverishness and all
you went through.   I say, have a look in this
drawer."

Waller thrust the open one in and pulled
out another.   " Look here, these are my old
nets with which we drag the hammer pond,
and catch the carp and tench ; great golden
fellows they are, some of them ; but the worst
of it is the pond's so deep that the fish dive
under the net and escape."

" And those which do not," said the lad

sadly, "you take in that net and make prisoners of them. Poor things! And what good are they to you when you have caught them?"

"Good? Good to eat! I say, what a fellow you are to talk of the fish one catches as prisoners! Carp and tench are not human beings."

"No, they are not human beings," said the lad, smiling sadly; "but they are prisoners, the same as I am."

"Oh, I say, what stuff! To call yourself a prisoner, when you are only a visitor here, and could come and go just as you like—at least, not quite, for it wouldn't be safe; but it will be soon."

"What's that coil of new rope for?"

"That?" cried Waller. "Oh, that's a new rope for my drag-net. The old one was quite worn out. You shall help me to fit this on if you like."

"Thank you. I'll help you if you wish."

"Well, I do wish, when you get well; but I don't care to see you in the dumps like this. Of course I know what it is: it's being shut up in this room for so long. A few good walks in the forest would make you as right as could be."

" Yes," said the lad wearily. " I feel as if I should like to be out again, for I often think when I am shut up here that it's like being a bird in a cage."

" Ah, you won't feel that long," said Waller.

It was the very next day when, after taking his new friend a selection of what he considered interesting books, Waller announced that he should not come upstairs again till the evening, for he had several things to do, and among others to write a letter to his father in London, and then take it to the village post-office for despatch.

" I don't think that either of the maids is likely to come up," said Waller, at parting ; " but if they should try the door, all you have got to do is to keep quite still. Of course, you will lock yourself in as soon as I am gone. Shall I bring you anything else to eat before I go ? "

" No," said the lad, with a weary look of disgust. " You bring me too much as it is ; more than I care to have. Don't bring me any more till I ask."

" I shall," said Waller, with a laugh. " I am not going to have you starve yourself to death up in my room. There, jump up and come and shut the door, and then have a good long read. I'll get back to you as soon as I can, and then we will have a good game at draughts or chess. But I mustn't be up here too much, or it will make the girls suspicious. There, good-bye for the present."

Waller went down and busied himself at once over the letter to his father, telling him of some of the things that were going on, but carefully—though strongly tempted— omitting all allusion to the fugitive.

It was rather a slow and laborious task for the boy, clever as he was at most things, though none too able in the use of a quill pen. But he got his letter finished at last, the big post-paper carefully folded and sealed, and then went off to the post-bag at the little village shop, before hurrying back home to partake of his tea, which was waiting.

It was a lonely meal, and the boy sighed as he stirred the sugar, and wished he could have Godfrey Boyne down, as companion for himself, and to cheer the poor fellow up.

It was quite dark by the time he had done, and with the full intention of suggesting that they should wait till the girls had gone to bed, and then steal down together for a walk in the forest, the boy rose to go and make an observation or two as to the position of the servants, before stealing up to join his friend.

Waller rose, went across to the bell, the pull of which he had taken in his hand, when he was startled by a distant scream, followed by half a dozen more, and the trampling of feet somewhere above, while, as he rushed out into the hall, he was just in time to hear a door bang and quick steps hurrying along the kitchen passage.

CHAPTER X.

ALARMING SOUNDS.

THE thoughts of Godfrey Boyne occupied so much position in Waller's brain that he at once concluded something must be wrong with him, and rushing upstairs two at a time, and making sure that he was not followed, he continued the rest of his way in the darkness as silently as he could, pausing to listen at the top of the attic stairs, and then cautiously creeping to and trying the door of his den.

All was perfectly still there, and he found the door fastened from within.

" False alarm," he said to himself ; and he crept down again to make his way to the kitchen, from which, as he drew nearer, there came faint hysterical cries and a most unpleasant smell of burning.

Hurrying into the kitchen, Waller found that the cries came from Bella, who was lying upon her back upon the shred hearthrug in front of the kitchen fire, while Martha was trying to bring her fellow-servant round from a fainting fit, and causing the horrible stench by burning the dried wing of a goose close to the girl's nostrils and making her sneeze violently.

" Oh dear ! Oh dear ! " cried Bella, uttering a sob, and then giving vent to a tremendous sneeze.

" Bless the King ! " said Martha Gusset quietly. " Sneeze again, dear ; it'll do you no end of good."

The advice came rather late, for the girl's face was already wrinkling up for another nervous convulson that seemed stronger than the last.

" Bless the King ! " said the cook again, " There, there, dear : you will be better soon."

" What's the matter, Martha ? " said Waller anxiously, and with a horrible dread upon him that all had been found out.

" She's had a fright, my dear. I don't quite know yet what it all means. She thinks she's seen something, but I daresay it's only one of them owls."

" Oh, no, no, no, no ! " sobbed Bella, " it was something dreadful—something dreadful ! "

" Well, well, then, my dear, tell us what it is," said Martha, in her most motherly way, " and it will do you good."

" Oh, it was dreadful ! " moaned Bella.

" I remembered that I had forgotten to shut the window in master's chamber, which I opened this afternoon to let the sun in and get the room aired, and without stopping to fetch a light I went up in the dark, and then— and then—Oh dear ! Oh dear ! Oh dear ! Oh dear ! "

" Take another sniff of the feathers, my dear, and have a good sneeze, and that will relieve you."

" Oh, do adone, cook, and throw the nasty thing behind the fire. I was just coming out again into the gallery, when I heard something horrid."

" Heard ? " cried Waller excitedly. " Then you didn't see it ? "

" No, Master Waller. I only heard it walking. Somewhere up by your room—I mean your den, as you call it. And then all in the dark there come *bumpity bump* all down the stairs, and I shruck and shruck again, and ran for my life."

" My ! " said cook. " Was it as bad as that ? But what was it, my dear ? "

" Oh, I don't know, cook. Something dreadfully horrid, and it was dragging a dead body all down the stairs, and knocking the back of the head hard on every step."

"Fancy!" said Martha, with an emphatic sniff. "It's all stuff, and nonsense. No such thing could have happened. It was all because you went up in the dark."

From feeling startled, and in dread of his secret being known, a rapid change came over Waller; half-suspecting what must have occurred, and finding it covered by the girl's superstitious notions, added to which there were the feathers, the sneezes, and the cook's blessings upon his Majesty King George III., the boy's risible faculties were so bestirred that he burst into a roar of laughter.

The effect was almost magical. Bella, who had been lying stretched out upon her back, tapping the floor with her heels occasionally in her paroxysms, suddenly started bolt upright, to exclaim in an indignant voice—

"Yes, it's all very fine for you to laugh, Master Waller!"

"Well, who wouldn't laugh at such non-sense?" said the boy.

"But it isn't nonsense, nor it isn't stuff, cook. You may laugh, sir, but there's some-thing walks up and down there in the dead of the night, and I heard it only last night, too, and told cook."

Martha Gusset slowly bent her head by
way of acquiescence, and made as if to throw
the goose-wing, with which she had been
fanning herself, behind the fire, but altered
her mind, and put it on the chimneypiece
with the bright brass candlesticks.

" Up and down where ? " asked Waller.

" Oh, I don't know, sir ; but it was somewhere in the roof."

" Bah ! " cried Waller, contemptuously.
" And pray what did cook say ? " he went on,
as he gave a glance at the comfortable-looking
dame.

" Said she was a silly goose, my dear," cried
the lady of the kitchen, with something like
a snort, " and that she mustn't eat so much
for supper. I told her, Master Waller, that
she might go up and down the stairs and
passages in the dead of the night for a hundred
years, and she'd never see anything uglier
than herself."

" Ah, you wait," said Bella.

" Did you hear or see anything, cook ? "
said Waller tentatively.

" I always go to bed to sleep," my dear.

" But I mean this evening, just now ? "

" No, my dear. I had had my tea, and
was having a comfortable nap over the fire."

" Why, Bella," said Waller, laughing, " you must have heard one of those big bouncing rats that make their nests in the ivy, and come in through the windows in the night."

" Ah, you may sneer at me, Master Waller, but I wouldn't sleep up there alone of a night for crowns of gold. It was just as I said. It was just like one of those horrid things you see in the old books in master's library, dragging dead bodies down the stairs."

" Rat dragging a dead sparrow," said Waller, and he hurried out of the kitchen to make his way out into the hall, where, consequent upon her fright, Bella had not lit the lamp, and then cautiously upstairs to the top attic, where he softly tried the door. He found it still fastened, and uttered a low signal agreed upon between the boys.

This was responded to by the click of the lock, and as Waller entered his fugitive guest went on tiptoe back to the old chair on which he passed so much of his time, and there was just faint light enough coming through the window to show that he was softly rubbing his back.

" What's the matter ? " said Waller.

" Fell down and hurt myself—all down those stairs. Made a big lump on my head."

" Why, what were you doing ? "

" Oh, I waited till it was growing dark, and then I felt that I must get out of this room, if only for a few moments, just to breathe the air in that big passage. But the steps were so horribly polished with wax that I went down from top to bottom."

" Oh ! " said Waller. " Then I suppose you don't know that you frightened one of our maids."

" Did I ? I think I did hear somebody shriek."

" You did ; and if you do things like that again, all will be found out. I shall get into terrible trouble, and you will be caught, and you know what that means."

" Yes," said Godfrey sadly ; " I know what that means."

" Well, then, I don't mean to trust you any more," said Waller, " and I shall keep that door locked until I feel it's safe. As soon as I can get you out, we will go off into the woods. I only hope our maid won't talk about it, but I am afraid she will."

There was cause for Waller's fear, for the very next day Bella told the gardener all about her alarm, and that night when he went down to the village shop, Joe Hanson made a small audience of the village people open their eyes widely, stare, and feel, as they told one another, a curious creepy sensation right down their backs.

One of the gardener's audience was Tony Gusset, a man who did not work much at shoe-making or mending, but when he did he thought a great deal, and after this occasion he mused much over what Bella had heard. Then he put that and that together, and thought of a certain reward of a hundred pounds for the taking, dead or alive, of any one of the French spies who had sought refuge in the forest ; and that reward haunted the village constable and kept him awake all night.

The next day, too, Bella's fright was food for reflection, and he mixed up with it the appearance of certain soldiers who had been billeted in the next village.

Tony Gusset thought very slowly, and he reasoned a good deal as well, and it resulted in his asking himself this question : If a man knew where the spies were and showed them to the soldiers, how much would he get, and how much would the soldiers want for their share ?

CHAPTER XI.

WEARY OF HIDING.

" IF he sees me going up and down like this he'll tell me I look like a wild beast in a cage, and he'll be quite right ; I do. I feel like one. There are moments when it seems as if I can't bear it. All this dreary wait, wait, wait ; all this longing to be out in the fresh air, free. It makes my head throb, and when he comes I could quarrel with him and fight, good chap as he is, so anxious to help me. And then there are the things he brings me. But I can't eat. I must—I will get out, if it's only for an hour's run so as to make myself tired. What must it feel to be a real prisoner, shut up, poor wretch, for years ! "

Godfrey Boyne, who looked thin and haggard still, was sitting upon the edge of the truckle bed, elbows on knees, chin upon one hand, while the nails of the other were brought close to his firm teeth, to be nibbled and gnawed down till they were close to the quick, as their owner gazed straight out through the open window at the remains of the glowing sunset, which were paling fast.

" Why hasn't he been to see me all these hours ? " he muttered. " He must know how dreary it is up here. He ought to have come. Books," he muttered, as he glanced sharply round, his eyes lighting for a moment upon one that lay open upon a chair ; " I couldn't read when it was all bright and light, and even if I could force myself to now, it will soon be dark. It was enough to make me angry and bang one book down, and throw the other in the corner. Hasn't he any brains ? To pick out such books as those— escapes from prison. Oh, how I should like to escape from mine and get into the woods ! He promised to take me. But, of course, I would come back. I wouldn't have Waller think me ungrateful for the world. I can't help liking him very much ; but he'd think it silly if I told him I did. He won't take me out to-night. He'd say again that it wasn't safe while the soldiers were about ; and I suppose he's right. Oh, how miserable it is ! I daren't even look out of the window for fear of being seen by the servants or the gardener. Well, it will soon be dark, and then I can stare out at the stars. I wonder whether father got away, and what he thinks about me. Let's see, how did that fellow escape ? "

he added, after an interval, during which dark clouds were sweeping up from the west, and the room seemed to fill with gloom. " Let's see, he made himself a rope."

A rope !

The lad sprang from his seat with the alacrity of a wild animal, for the very mention of a rope gave full play to his imagination, and sent him hurrying to and fro to the full extent of what he looked upon as his cage.

The next moment he was down upon his knees dragging out one of the drawers which contained his young host's treasures. In an instant the great tangle of fine meshes, pike-shaped leads, and strung-together corks was thrust on one side, while, with a faint sigh of exultation, the prisoner drew out the coil of light brown, pleasant-smelling, firmly twisted hemp that had been intended to form the new drag-rope of the net.

" Hah ! " panted the lad, as he threw the coil like a great quoit upon the quilt, and then thrust in the drawer.

The next minute he was seated upon the edge of the bed with the rope in his lap, and busily untying the string that, in three places, secured it in shape, for it was brand new, just as it had come from the ship chandler's in Southampton City.

This was soon done, the stiff rope beginning to expand its rings as if it were some live serpent-like creature eager to escape from its bonds. But Godfrey Boyne paid no heed to this, not even once thinking of coiling it up again and replacing it in the drawer, for, as he thought hard, breathed hard, and felt his spirits expanding like the rope at the thoughts of being free, he saw in imagination the deep dark forest glades, felt the mossy, springy turf beneath his feet, and gave way to that strange half-wild excitement which comes at times upon a boy, and sets him bounding off like some wild creature of the plains, to run, and run, and run onward for no reason at all, until he is forced to stop for want of breath.

" Oh, yes," he muttered, " I can fasten it to that beam, slide down, have my run, and get back again without Waller knowing ; and I will. No one shall see me. I'll take care of that."

The thought of being at last in action sent a thrill through the lad's breast, as if he had taken some powerful tonic, while, as if Nature was completely transforming him, he sprang up again, laying the cord upon the bed, and began to pace the sloping-ceiled room once more.

It seemed as if Nature were favouring him further, for the darkness came on like magic till there was quite obscurity enough to favour his designs, and, going straight to the window he thrust out his head.

"He will not be up till after he has had his supper, and I could have a couple of hours' run before then," thought the boy; and, leaning out, he plunged his hands into the thick ivy.

"What do I want with a rope?" he muttered. "I could climb down here by holding on to these tough stems. Any of these are strong enough to bear me, and——"

Crack!

The tuft of green growth he was holding and involuntarily pressing hard, snapped off short and fell to the ground, rustling softly as it passed over the projecting strands.

Godfrey Boyne shook his head and laughed.

"I should get down quickly enough," he said to himself, "but what about getting back?"

Drawing in his head, he felt for—as it was getting very dark—one end of the thin rope, and then, mounting a stool, he passed the strong hempen twist over the beam, which just allowed room for it to pass, knotted the end, made a slip noose, drew it tight, and then, feeling for the other end of the coil, he began to run it out through the open dormer, listening with wild exultation to the passage of this narrow high-road to liberty over the rustling ivy.

It was all excitement now. There was no room for hesitation, as, passing one leg out of the window, holding on to the centre support the while, he drew out the other, lowered himself a little, reaching out with his feet so as to get them beyond the stone gutter below, and then, seizing the rope, he twined one leg round it and began to let himself slide.

But it was not done without noise. The twigs of ivy, as he passed over and through them, crackled and snapped ; while, as he slid down more and more, and the projecting gutter held the rope out clear, he began to perform evolutions like those of a leg of mutton, pendent from a roasting-jack, the rope displaying more and more desire to untwine.

Gripping it tightly, and using his other leg as a break against further descent, Godfrey stopped short to listen, and as he did so he suffered from a catching of the breath, for all at once he heard a sound from within the house, the ivy on a level with his face became illuminated, and a candle was carried past the window of the room by which he swung.

He had a glimpse of a woman's face, and as he felt convinced by the gleam of her eyes that she must see him, the light grew less, and was gone.

The next minute the lad, after a few more evolutions that threatened to make him giddy, felt his feet touch the soft earth of a flower-bed, from which he swung himself on to the lawn, and was feeling about for the loose rope finding that there were at least twenty yards lying about amongst the shrubs.

These he gathered together into one spot, and, with a feeling of exultation growing in his sense of freedom, he gave a sharp glance through the darkness to right and left, and then, making for the carriage-drive, whose position he fully knew now, he strode off rapidly and silently in the direction of one of the forest paths which led towards the little village; but of this fact he was naturally unaware.

CHAPTER XII.

AN ADVENTURE.

GODFREY BOYNE, consequent upon the darkness, was forced to keep to the well-beaten road ; but it was grand.   He breathed freely ; there was a feeling of exultation to make his chest expand ; his nostrils quivered with the delight he felt ; and from time to time he checked his strong desire to run, and stopped to listen to the sounds that arrested his attention on either side—sometimes soft and mysterious, sometimes startling.

There was the low rustling amongst last year's leaves as some mouse was busy. Then the faint trickling of a worm struggling with a strand which it was fighting hard to drag into its hole.

A little farther on he was startled by a sudden rush as something bounded away from close to his feet ; and, as he stood breathing hard, he could hear it go on *pat, pat, pat, pat,* right away, till the sounds died out.

He knew it was a rabbit, but the suddenness made his heart beat faster all the same.

Then he was off again, to startle—as he had been startled himself—a blackbird or thrush suddenly awakened from its roost, or hear the loud flapping of a woodpigeon beating through the trees overhead.

There were other sounds, too, to which he could not give a name. But it was all dark, mysterious, and delightful, as he went on cautiously lest he should lose touch of the road, and find difficulty in getting back.

How long this lasted, or how far he had gone, was driven out of his mind soon after, when he came to a sudden turn in the wood where something dimly seen glided by him, close to his face, uttering a most unearthly shriek which, to use the common expression, brought his heart to his mouth and seemed to fix his feet to the ground.

Then it was gone, gliding away upon silent wing, and he had sufficient commonsense to attribute the sound to a screech-owl.

" Not one of those," he muttered, " that hoot and shout and answer one another as they fly round the house at night. There," he said, with a sigh, " I won't stop any longer. I don't know how long I have been, but I don't want Waller to find me out. He wouldn't like it ; and it doesn't seem right."

He stopped, hesitating now, the incident of the passing owl that he had come upon, and startled into uttering its shriek of dread on finding itself suddenly in such close contact with its great enemy, man, having confused him a little as to his direction, and it was some moments before he was sure of his road.

But he was taking the right course, and, feeling more himself, less morbid and nervous, refreshed as he was by the exercise, interest, and pure fresh air, he reached the gate at the end of the drive, passed on up into the grounds and, during the latter part of his return journey, was guided by the light in the porch and in the dining-room window.

· " It was all so easy," he said to himself, " and I could do it again at any time. But no ; I won't. I won't give way to those feelings. It's ungenerous to Waller, and he is such a good fellow. I am sure he likes me, and I want to be grateful and like him too. If he found me out I should lose his respect and confidence."

These were the lad's last thoughts in this direction, for he had reached the lawn, over which he passed lightly, and began feeling about for the rope.

Then his heart seemed to stand still, and a choking feeling assailed him, for the rope was gone—only for a few moments, for as he roused himself to action, and mastered his feeling of dismay, he awoke to the fact that he was feeling beneath the wrong window. Then a few yards to his right his searching hand came in contact with the firm twisted cord, which he grasped with both hands as high up as he could reach, drew up his legs to get the rope twisted round, and then began to —climb ? No—gently swing to and fro. It was a very pleasant motion as he brushed against the shrubs and once bumped up against the sill of one of the lower windows, but it was not what he wanted.

For the first time in his life he was realising that, though it is very easy to slide down a rope, it is quite a gymnastic feat, only to be mastered by long practice, to climb up a cord that is comparatively slight.

" Oh, why didn't I remember to make a knot at every foot ? " thought the lad, as he severely abused himself for his folly and ignorance during the intervals of struggling hard to get, if only a few feet up, towards the window, but toiling in vain and only growing hotter and more exhausted in spite of all.

He rested for a while, and once more tried, rested, and tried again, and at last, utterly fagged out, he gave up in despair.

He was so wearied out that, still holding by the rope, he sank upon his knees amongst the shrubs that dotted the broad bed beneath the windows, and even when his breath was coming easily once more, and the hot burning pain in his chest had subsided, the spirit to make another attempt was wanting, and, with a feeling of despair increasing, he began to plan what he should do till morning— whether he could get round to the back and find an entrance to the stables and pass the night in a loft, so as to try and steal in some time in the morning, and reach the attic unseen.

"But Waller will be going up and finding that I am gone," he thought. "He will see the rope hanging out of the window, and—— Oh, what an idiot I have been ! If I had only waited and been patient for another day or two, perhaps——" He stopped short, for he was conscious of what sounded like a deep sigh close at hand, then of a heavy stertorous breathing, and, dimly seen, not a couple of yards away, he made out the shape of a big, heavy, stooping man, passing over the lawn very slowly, and as if looking for him. For that was the only interpretation that he could place upon the man's movements.

It was not Waller, nor the gardener, for certain ; but who it could be, in his excitement, he could not hazard a conjecture. He himself was fugitive and spy, and the only interpretation natural was that this man was hunting for him, and he was lost.

So startled was the boy by the adventure, so exhausted by what he had gone through, that it never occurred to him to make a dash for liberty. He crouched there, literally paralysed, and for the moment he could not believe it true that, due to his silence and position, he was unseen, and the man had passed away into the darkness, and his heavy panting breath had died away. In the reaction came the thought of what he ought to do, and with it the wonder that it had not occurred to him before.

Pausing a few brief moments to make sure that he was quite alone, Godfrey rose from his crouching position, and, with the rope gliding through his hand, he stepped outward on to the lawn at right-angles to the front of the house, to feel the next minute the sharp needles of the big fir-tree brushing his face and making a crickling, crackling noise as the rope, which passed through his hands, rustled among the boughs.

The next minute he had forced his way in close up to the trunk, and, running the rope through his hands, till he got hold of the free end, he fastened it round his waist and then began to climb.

It would have been easy enough getting from bough to bough, which stood straight out, and was facile for one who mounted as if he were going up a ladder ; but there was the rope, which kept catching and the noise it made as he had to shake and snatch to free it in its passage amongst the lower branches.

But he persevered, and climbed and climbed with his task growing lighter, the branches thinner, and he found himself right up the grand old tree, which towered above the roof, leaving him now on a level with the window from which he had lowered himself.

Godfrey paused, breathless, with one arm round a horizontal branch to rest himself a little and listen ; but all was still, and, un-tying the rope from about his waist, he passed it round the tree, a comparatively easy task now, for, embracing the trunk, his hands touched, and directly after he was hauling upon the rope, had drawn it tight, so tight that it was pretty well horizontal, when, passing it round the trunk again, he notted it firmly, forming a spider line ready for him to creep along to his sanctuary in the roof.

It required a little nerve, but the lad was desperate, and, trusting to his knots at either end being firm, he took hold of the rope, let his feet glide down, and then began to travel hand over hand, swinging more and more till his feet ceased to touch the nearest boughs, when, throwing them up, he hooked first one leg and then the other over the giving rope, and, relieving the weight upon his arms, began to creep more quickly over the ten or fifteen yards which separated the tree-trunk from the house.

The rope, in spite of his efforts to tighten it, formed a deep bow as he went along, easily at first, but with the difficulty increasing as the depth of the curve was passed, and the latter part was somewhat of a climb,

But almost before he could realise it, he was passing through the window with his eyes closed, and his first intimation of the success of his scheme was given by his right hand touching the knot which attached the rope to the attic beam.

Dropping his feet to the floor, and trembling violently with excitement and exertion, the lad took a step to the window and peered out, listening ; but all was still, and, taking his knife from his pocket, he felt for, and mounted the stool again, sawed through the rope, and, twisting it up till he had it tight from the tree, he leaned out, pulled hard once more so as to get the spring of the fir, and then threw it with all his might.

There was a faint rustle as, helped by the bend given to the upper part of the trunk, the rope left his hand and fell amongst the needle-covered boughs, and then, closing the window, the lad, panting more from excitement than exertion, crept to the door and listened till, making sure that he heard Waller's step below, he rushed to the bed, dragged down the clothes, sprang in, drew them up to his chin, and then, with his face to the wall, lay with closed eyes, striving hard to subdue the heaving of his breast.

CHAPTER XIII.

A REPRIMAND.

GODFREY, as it happened, had time for his excitement to calm down, for, after listening intently for Waller's foot upon the last flight of stairs, one of which always gave out a now familiar crack, he found that he had allowed his imagination to invent, for he had not heard his companion coming up. In fact, a good ten minutes elapsed, during which the silence was profound, and, growing hotter than ever, lying there beneath the clothes, fully dressed, and after going through a great deal of exertion, the listener half raised himself to get out, either to undress or to sit down calmly and wait.

He was hesitating which to do, when there now came that unmistakable crack which made him nestle down in the bed again, and draw the clothes to his chin, just as there was the sharp rattle of the key in the door. This was flung open, and Waller sprang in, to dash through the darkness and thrust his head out of the window and look down into the gloom beneath. Drawing back directly, he faced inwards.

"Godfrey," he whispered sharply, "where are you ? Are you there ?"

There was no reply.

"Do you hear ?" whispered Waller, a little more loudly. "Where are you ? What have you been up to ?"

Still no reply, and the boy crossed quickly to place his hand upon the bed, and say, in an excited whisper as if relieved by what he had found—

"Oh, you are here. I thought you had gone. You can't be asleep. Why don't you speak ? There," he cried, loudly now, "you are shamming !" For his hands had been travelling over the clothes. "Why, you are dressed ! There, out you come !" And catching hold of the coverlet, he stripped everything right down to the foot.

Startled at this unexpected action, Godfrey sprang up, and, with hands rapidly following the gliding clothes, he seized them, threw himself back, and dragged them up to his chin again.

"There, I knew you were shamming ! What game have you been up to ?"

"Eh ? What ?" faltered the lad, trying

to speak as if he were confused. " Is anything the matter ?   Have the soldiers come ?"

" No," cried Waller hotly, " but I have.
There, it's no use to try and keep up that
sham. What have you been doing ? You
may just as well confess. There, you have
got your boots on, too. You have not been
doing that for nothing."

" What do you mean ? "

" That you are trying to hide something,
and you only got into bed to hide it when you
heard me coming. What have you been
doing ? "

" What have I been doing ? "

" Yes. I know."

Godfrey was silent.

" I did trust you. Thought you wouldn't
attempt to do anything without confiding in
me. You have been trying to do something
with the rope."

" Well," said Godfrey sourly, " suppose I
have ! What then ? And how did you know ?"

" How did I know ? Why, I was just
taking a walk round outside, and I thought
I'd have a look up at your window, and I
don't know how it was, but I seemed to have
a fancy that you had been striking a light,
and had got a candle burning ; and that

meant for one of the servants to see, perhaps
Joe Hanson, when they all knew that I was
downstairs. You did'nt do such a mad thing,
did you ?

" No, of course not," said Godfrey sulkily.

" Then what did you do ? "

" What do you mean ? "

" What do I mean ? What made you
throw a rope out of the window so that the
end of it hit me right across the head ? What
rope was it ? How came you by it ? Oh ! "
The boy dashed to the great press, pulled out
one of the lower drawers, and thrust in his
hand. " I thought so ! You have been
getting out that coil to fasten it to the window,
and let it slip."

Godfrey was silent.

" Do you know the end of that hit me
right across the head when you dropped
it ? "

Still no answer.

" How I could have been so stupid as to
let you see, I don't know. Why, you meant
to go off on the sly by yourself. Were you
going to run right away ? "

" No," replied Godfrey. " There, I'll tell
you. I couldn't bear it any longer. It
was so dreadful being shut up, and I only

wanted to go and have a walk in the woods. I meant to come up again."

" And you let the rope slip, and lost it. Lucky for you. Do you know what it meant ? You being strange to this place, and not knowing which way to go, either losing yourself in the dark, or else blundering into the village, where you would have been seen by some one. Why, the chances are that you would have blundered up against Joe Hanson, who generally goes round of a night seeing that the fowls are all right and no fox about after the ducks. I call it too bad, Godfrey, when I have been trying so hard to keep you safe until we can hear that the soldiers are gone. Now, I say, why don't you confide in me as you should ? Don't you believe in me ? "

" Yes, thoroughly," said Godfrey, sadly, as he stretched out his hand in Waller's direction, touched him on the arm, and began to slide his fingers down till they touched his hand ; but Waller shrank away.

" You don't trust me," he said, " and I shan't trust you."

" There, I'll confess all about it," said the lad, in a low, husky tone. " I know now it was half mad of me, but I couldn't bear the

silence and loneliness any more. I felt that
I must go and breathe the fresh night air
somehow, and so I fastened the rope and slid
down and went and had a walk. It was after
I had got back again," he continued hurriedly,
feeling too shamefaced to relate all the facts,
" that I threw the rope out of the window ;
and then you came up suddenly, and I felt
so guilty that I pretended I had gone to bed."

" Just like a naughty little boy who knew
that he had done something wrong," said
Waller bitterly. " I wouldn't have believed
that a young fellow like you, almost a man,
would have acted like a child."

" Don't be hard on me, Waller. You
don't know what I suffered. You can't
think what it is to be a prisoner like this."

" No, and I can't think what made you
act as you did. I can't understand how you
managed to climb up again. But why did
you chuck the rope out of the window ? You
couldn't have heard me coming then."

" No," said Godfrey ; and then it all came
out.

" Oh," said Waller, " of course that was
a white owl ; but it was just as I told you.
Old Joe does make a snoring sort of noise
when he has been walking fast or mowing,

and he was prowling round before he went
back to the cottage, and looking to see if
Bella had shut all the windows. He's rather
fond of catching her out in forgetting them,
and then he comes and tells tales, and they
quarrel. Joe has got pretty sharp eyes, and
you must have sat there squat or else he'd
have seen you. Well, I suppose I must
forgive you, but you had a very narrow
escape. Do you know what this means ? "

" Yes ; as you say, that you will forgive
me, and we are going to be friends again."

" Yes, but something more. That I must
be up before daybreak, go to the tool-house
for a rake, and smooth over your footsteps in
the long bed under the windows, and after
that, get up the old fir-tree and pull down the
rope. I almost wonder that you didn't
break your neck. You must have been half-
mad, old fellow."

" Yes," said Godfrey, with a sigh, " I must
indeed."

CHAPTER XIV

THE SEARCH.

GODFREY started up from a deep sleep, to see it was morning with the sun shining brightly, and that the birds were singing, while Waller was standing by his bedside smiling at him as he looked at him wonderingly, and apparently quite confused.

" Come, old fellow, wake up," said Waller. " I have been up two hours."

" Up two hours ! I—— there's nothing wrong, is there ? "

" Wrong ? No. You are always thinking some one's coming after you. It's all right."

." But I don't understand," said Godfrey.

" Why, you don't mean to say you've forgotten all about last night ? "

" Last night ! " cried the lad, with a start.

" Oh, I had forgotten. No ; I was not quite awake. You have been up early to go and get that rope."

Waller pointed to the big, old easy chair.

" Does seem like it, doesn't it ? There it is, all soaked with dew. I soon got it down, and I have been busy over the bed. You had trampled it terribly. and there were two great bits of ivy snapped off as well and lying there. I've made it pretty tidy, and there has been such a heavy due that your footprints on the grass, and those of Joe Hanson, going round the house, are pretty well taken out. They'll be all right now, I think."

" Oh, thank you," cried Godfrey, with a sigh ; " but now, I suppose, I must give up all hope of going into the woods with you again."

" Nonsense ! I only want you to wait till it's sensible to go."

" Ah ! " cried Godfrey. " I like to hear you talk so. Do you know, I was dreaming this morning about what you said the other day."

" What was that ? "

" About getting me down to Lymington, and on board a fishing-boat."

" And so I will."

" Thank you. Then we will start to-night."

" That we won't ! " cried Waller. " Stuff ! Nonsense ! I hear from our gardener that there are soldiers going about from place to place in the forest, and as likely as not we should run right up against them, for they would be sure to be keeping watch at night. You wait a bit, and as soon as I think it's safe, and we have made all our plans, we will go. But don't you be in such a hurry. You are company for me, and I am sure my father wouldn't mind your staying on a while to get strong. I want to hear that the soldiers are gone, and then you will be like a visitor, and we will have a good time of it in the woods, fishing, and collecting, and one thing and another."

" No," said the lad sadly ; " England is no place for me. I must get back to France."

" You wait till you get better," said Waller, " and you will talk differently."

" Oh, but I am putting you in such a false position. Your servants will be finding out that you have got me hidden here."

" They'd better ! " cried Waller hotly. " What business is it of theirs ? I am only answerable to my father."

" And what will he say to you when he knows what you have done ? "

" What will he say ? " cried Waller enthusiastically. " He'll say—he'll say—I don't know what," and the boy stopped short.

Another day elapsed, and Waller was chatting eagerly with his prisoner, and planning with him that they should steal out as soon as it was dusk, and go and have a ramble in the woods.

" But it will be dark," said Boyne wearily.

" There," cried Waller, " you are speaking as dumpily as you did when we first met. That means that you ought to be out in the fresh air. Of course it will be dark. No, it won't, because there will be some moon to-night ; and if it were dark it wouldn't matter. There's always something to hear, with the creatures in the forest hunting— owls, and stoats, and all sorts of night things. Why, I can find my way anywhere nearly in the forest of a night. You don't know what fun it is till you get out there. I have been out with Bunny Wrigg sometimes when he has been setting night-lines in the old hammer pond, and catching big eels, and sometimes wild ducks, and——Pst ! Someone coming ! "

" Master Waller, are you upstairs ? " came from below ; and the boy pressed his finger on his lips and took a little saw from where it was hanging against the wall, put it down noisily, and picked up a hammer from where it lay upon a bench-like table.

The next moment he was tapping a box softly, as if he were driving in a nail, while the uncarpeted stairs leading to the attic creaked, and the light step of the girl was heard coming towards the door.

Next moment she was knocking sharply.

" Master Waller ! Master Waller ! " she cried excitedly. " You must come down directly ; you are wanted."

" Eh ? "cried the boy. " Who wants me ? "

" There's Tony Gusset, sir, Martha's brother, and he's come along with six soldiers."

Waller sprang from his seat, striking the table a heavy blow with the hammer in his excitement as he rose, while his companion, who had followed the example, took a couple of steps towards the open dormer window, and stood there with his lips pinched together and hands clenched.

" What do they want ? " cried Waller sharply, as he caught his companion by the wrist.

" They are coming to search the house, sir."

" What ? " shouted Waller hoarsely.

" Coming to hunt for spies, sir."

Waller drew a deep breath as if pulling

himself together to face the desperate position, and his companion looked at him wonderingly as he called out, in a voice full of assumed bravado ;

" Oh, are they？ I will come down to see about that ! "

" Yes, sir, do, please. Martha's in such a way, and she's quarrelling with her brother awful."

" Go on down ! " cried Waller, and he gave the table a heavy thump with his hammer before listening to the girl's descending steps, and breathing hard as if he had been running the while.

As the girl's steps died out he faced round to look in the fugitive's eyes. There was a faint smile on the lad's lips as he caught Waller's hand and gripped it fast.

" Thank you," he said very calmly. " It's all over, Waller—brother Waller. There, I am going to meet it like a man."

" What ! " said Waller, in a hoarse whisper, as if he thought their words might be heard through the open window. " What are you going to do ? "

" Surrender," was the reply, " and take care that you come to no harm for harbouring me here."

Waller laughed mockingly, as he snatched away his hand and clapped it and its fellow upon the other's shoulders.

" You've been too long in France," he whispered. " An English boy would not give up like that. Never say die ! "

" What do you mean ? " panted the other, startled by Waller's earnestness.

" To dodge these bloodhounds, as you call . them, and give them the slip ; and as for old bumpy Gusset, this is his doing, because he's got a spite against father, and if you and I don't serve him out for it, my name's not Waller Froy. Pst ! " he whispered, with his lips close to the other's ear. " Don't make a rustle nor a sound," he continued, after whispering for a few moments, " and never stir. I'll send them about their business, never fear."

Short as was the time that this interchange of words had taken, it was too long, for loud, hoarse voices were heard as of men assembling in the hall, and, giving his companion an encouraging slap upon the back, Waller dashed out of the room, banged to the door, locked it, and thrust the key into his pocket, keeping his hand there as he carelessly made for the staircase, descended to the gallery, and the next minute was looking over the broad balustrade down into the hall, where a couple of soldiers stood, with grounded muskets, staring through the dining-room door, while another was in the porch on guard, and voices came from out of the room.

" Hullo ! " shouted Waller to the two soldiers, who had turned to look at him directly. " Who are you, and what do you want ? "

Without waiting for an answer he took a couple of steps, threw himself on to the great carved balustrade, and, rapidly gliding down upon his chest, literally shot off before he reached the upright scroll at the bottom. and faced the men. His loud questioning voice brought out a sergeant, musket in hand, and sword and bayonet in his diagonal belt behind, closely followed by a big, fat, puffy, unwholesome-looking man with sallow face and baggy eyes.

CHAPTER XV.

THE SEARCH CONTINUED.

THE man had on a cobbler's leather apron, which he had rolled up and tucked in the strap. He had pulled on his jacket, but evidently without turning down the sleeves of his shirt, which showed through just beneath his shoulders in two rolls like mock muscles, while a very much battered felt hat, with a flap looped up to form three cocks, was worn jauntily upon his head.

" Morning, sir," said the sergeant, looking the boy up and down sharply. " Are you Squire Froy ? "

" No, I am his son," said Waller haughtily, as he strode past the stiff-looking military man so as to bring himself within arm's length of the cobbler, and, with a movement quick as a flash, struck off his cocked hat and sent it flying. " What do you mean by that, sir ? " he shouted at him. " Is that the way to enter a gentleman's house ? " and with a half-run across the echoing polished oak boards he made a kick at the hat, and, to the great delight of the soldiers, sent it flying out through the porch.

" If you weren't an old man I'd kick you, too," he continued, as the astounded constable dressed in a little brief authority, opened his mouth like a carp, too much amazed to speak. " You would have come sneaking round to the back door if my father had been at home, or else have stood wiping your dirty shoes upon the mat." Then, turning his back upon the man he addressed, he faced the leader of the soldiers. " Now, sergeant," he said, " what's the meaning of this intrusion ? "

There was a good deal of the cock bantam about the boy's ways and speech, but it was manly all the same. He had real authority, too, for speaking out to the rough, coarse-looking villager, and with quick military precision the sergeant, whose eyes sparkled on hearing his rank acknowledged, saluted sharply.

" Beg pardon, sir ; on duty," he said. " Me and my men, we are in search of French spies who are loose somewhere about the forest, and this man from down the village tells me that one or two of them are likely to be harboured here. Not a pleasant job, sir, but I am only obeying orders, and we shall have to search the place."

" Search the place ! " cried Waller hotly.

" Yes, sir, in the King's name."

" Oh," said Waller cooly, as he darted a furious glance at Gusset, who was still opening and shutting his mouth without making a sound ; and then, noting that Martha and Bella had come to the door leading to the servants' offices, and were looking on, while the gardener, bearing his scythe, had come round to the porch, to be stopped by the soldier placed as sentry, who held his musket across the man's chest, " In the King's name, eh ? " said Waller coolly.

" Yes, sir. Very sorry, but my duty."

" Oh, well, I am not going to blame you," said Waller ; " but I should have thought as my father is a county magistrate this house ought to be respected."

" Yes, sir, of course," said the sergeant ; " but don't you see, it's like protecting him against the French."

" Search away, then," cried Waller, " and when you have done—here, Martha ! "

" Yes, sir," came from the door.

" Don't let these soldiers go away without giving them a crust of bread and cheese."

"No, sir; I'll have it ready directly," cried Martha; and then, in a whisper to her fellow-servant, "Bless the boy! Don't he speak up like a man!"

"Where are you going to begin, sergeant?"

"Thank you, sir, for the lunch," said the sergeant, smiling; and he gave the lad another admiring look—one that took him in from top to toe, while his eyes seemed to speak the thoughts of his heart. "What a smart young officer he'd make! Shouldn't I like the job of drilling him into shape!"

"Oh, we will begin at the bottom, sir, and search to the top."

"But suppose there are Frenchmen here," said Waller, laughing, "why, they might be getting away into the woods while you are talking!"

"Not they, sir," said the man, with a cunning smile. "I have got a man at each door as sentry, and two more on vedette back and front. Not much fear of that."

"But suppose they make a bolt, like the rabbits do in the forest," said Waller.

"Bad for them if they did, sir," replied the sergeant, rather sternly. "My men can shoot."

Waller whistled softly.

" Oh, ho ! " he said ; and he tapped the barrel of the sergeant's musket with his knuckles. " Loaded ? "

The man gave him a quiet nod.

"Go on, then ; search away, and get it done. You have been in the dining-room, I see."

The village constable, who had been listening, with his eyes starting and ears seeming to project forward, here broke in, speaking in a husky, oily voice.

" Big cellar, sergeant, all underneath the house, and iron gratings to let in the light."

"What do you know about it ? " cried Waller sharply. " Have you been prying and peering in ? "

" I am a-doin' of my duty, Master Waller Froy," said the man, swelling up like a turkey-cock, which bird he seemed greatly to resemble as, having found his voice, he began to show his importance, but with no other effect than to make the soldiers grin, while one of them, who had walked out past the sentry and picked up the cocked hat with the muzzle of his musket, now presented it to him.

" Don't—don't do that ! " cried the constable, starting back as if it were something alive. " You should never point a gun at anyone when you speak ! "

" Didn't speak," said the soldier, grinning more widely.

" There, take your hat, constable," cried the sergeant, giving Waller a comical cock of his eye. " Brown Bess never barks unless we touch the trigger. Yes, sir, I have looked through the dining-room. Beautiful old-fashioned room, too. Excuse me for saying so. No secret passages there, I suppose ? "

" No," said Waller ; " not one. Come and look here, then, next. I'll take you wherever you want to go. This is the drawing-room," and he threw open the door of the handsome low-ceilinged, old panelled chamber, with most of the furniture dating back so that it was nearly as old as the house.

As he led the way into the room Waller winced, for Anthony Gusset was putting on his cocked hat again ; but as he caught the boy's furious look he snatched it off.

" Look here, sergeant," said Waller quietly ; " I'll take you all over the house and answer any questions you like to put, or won't answer them, just as I please, but you can do your duty without that fat, stupid, village bumpkin ? "

" To be sure I can, sir. Here, you, constable, stop there with my sentry at the
porch, and if you see a Frenchman bolt, you
shout."

As he spoke, the man backed Gusset into
the hall, for he was following into the drawing-
room, making him open his thick lips in fish
like fashion once again as if to speak ; but a
prod in the ribs given by the sergeant's fore-
finger forced obedience, and he went out
unwillingly into the porch.

The sergeant returned to Waller, who was
standing in the middle of the room with
his hands in his pockets, whistling an old
country ditty softly, while the two soldiers
made a pretence of searching the room,
and then looked for orders from their
officer.

" You haven't looked up the chimney,
my lads," cried Waller, laughing. " Oh, you
needn't stare ; there's plenty of room in it
for a horse to get up," and he laughingly
stepped forward into the wide chimney-
corner. " Look here, officer, you don't often
see a place like this."

" My word, no, sir ! " said the sergeant,
stooping down and following Waller into the
great wide place. " They used to build in

the old days, and make room for the smoke. Why, the ivy's hanging right down through the top."

" Yes," said Waller : " plenty of ivy here. Now you'd like to see the library ? "

This was looked into, and then a slight search was made of what Waller called the schoolroom, and a little, old-fashioned boudoir.

" That's all here," said the boy, " except the servant's places."

" What about the cellar, sir ? " said the sergeant.

" Oh, we'll go into that through the outer hall," and, Waller, leading the way, the searchers passed through the various offices, and, on lights being provided and a big key being fetched from the squire's study table, the big, crypt-like, vaulted cellars were searched from end to end. Lastly, Waller led the way upstairs to the gallery, where the oaken polished floor echoed to the soldiers' heavy tread.

" Where does that staircase lead, sir ? " said the sergeant, as his task drew near its end.

" Attics in the roof," said Waller. " Up you go."

" Well, sir, I am getting rather tired of this job," said the man, hesitating.

" Oh, but you have got it to do. Finish it off," said Waller carelessly ; and he made way for the soldiers to pass up, and stood below swinging himself to and fro, balancing himself toe and heel.

" Come on, my lads," said the sergeant. " Forward, and be smart. I am thinking that crust of bread and cheese must be ready by now."

The men laughed good-humouredly, and the bare staircase creaked and groaned beneath their heavy tread, which directly afterwards made the upper passage, with its sloping ceiling, which followed the shapes of the gables, echo.

That part of the search was quickly done, not so quickly that it did not give time to Waller to whistle the stave of the old Hampshire ditty three times over.

He had just got to the last bar for this third time when the butt of the sergeant's musket was dropped with a heavy bang upon the floor overhead.

" Beg pardon, sir," he shouted down to Waller. " There's one of these 'ere doors locked ! "

"Eh?" cried Waller, whose face now looked scarlet, and who stood for a moment or two holding his breath.

"One door here locked, sir. I ought to see into every room."

"Oh, to be sure! That's my den," cried the boy cavalierly—"my workshop. I am coming," and springing up two steps at a time he faced the sergeant, who, with two men, was waiting by the locked door.

Waller thrust his hand into his pocket, and the sergeant looked at him sharply, for his breath, possibly from · the exertion, came thick and fast, while the key seemed to stick in his pocket as if it had got across.

"There you are," he said jauntily. "It's full of my rubbish and odds and ends. Catch!"

He pitched the key, and the sergeant caught it with one hand as cleverly as if he had been a cricketer, turned, and began to insert it in the lock.

"Mind the snakes!" cried Waller mockingly; while, in spite of a strong effort, he felt half choked, and his voice sounded strained and hard.

"Snakes?" said the sergeant, pausing with the key half turned. "Up here?"

" Yes," said Waller ; " at least a dozen. I am a collector, you know."

The sergeant gave him a searching look, hesitated a moment, and then, with a half-smile upon his lip, he turned the key. The bolt flew back with a sharp snap and he threw open the door.

CHAPTER XVI.

STILL SEARCHING.

WITH a mingling of instinct and the practice of the profession, the sergeant's two followers brought down their muskets to the present as the door flew wide, presumably to meet the attack of the snakes, but the curled and dried-up skins, so light without the sand that a sharp puff of wind would have blown them away, lay still upon the shelf, and there was no rush for escape made by Godfrey Boyne. The place, full of its litter of odds and ends dear to the young naturalist, and with its open windows, lay open to the gaze of the soldiers, and the sergeant, after a sharp look round, which satisfied him that the place was empty, turned to Waller.

" I thought it meant game, sir," he said. " Where's your sarpints ? "

" Yonder on the shelf," said Waller, with a mischievous look in his eyes.

" Yah ! Stuffed ! Well, sir, we have done ; and thank you for being so nice to us over an unpleasant job."

" Oh, don't name it, sergeant," said Waller cooly.

" Right about face, my lads ! Forward ! March !—Halt !—About that there window— how far is it to the ground ? "

" Oh, nice little jump," said Waller coolly. " About thirty feet, I suppose."

But though he spoke calmly there was a curious twitching at the corners of the boy's eyes and his nether lip seemed to quiver as the stiff, keen-looking man marched to the casement and leaned out, looking sharply to right and left.

" Don't see any bits, sir, lying below," he said with a grim laugh. " No one seems to have jumped out there. My word ! You grow a fine lot of ivy about this house, but I suppose it wasn't planted yesterday.—Now, then, forward, my lads ! " he continued ; and then, with a laugh and a nod to Waller, he jerked his right thumb in the direction of the men. " They are not thinking of catching spies, sir, but about that bread and cheese."

" Ah, well, they shall have it as soon as you have done," said Waller, the nerves of whose face had ceased to twitch.

" Oh, we have done, sir," said the man,

" and glad of it. This is not the sort of thing I like. Don't seem proper work for soldiers. I have done, sir, unless you have any other place you want us to search."

" Oh, not I," said Waller. " I shall be glad to see your backs."

The men began to descend, while Waller carefully locked the door and pocketed his key.

" I don't like servants to meddle with my knick-knacks," he said.

" Of course you don't, sir. I used to be very fond of that sort of thing when I was a boy, in Devon."

The next minute they were down in the fine old entrance-hall, to be met by Gusset, who bustled forward out of the porch with his protruding eyes rolling a little as he stared hard at the sergeant, and then, mis-judging a movement on the part of Waller, he snatched off his hat.

" You ar'nt found them, then ? " he said to the sergeant.

" No, constable ; there's no spy here, French or English. It's all a mare's nest, and you have brought us for nothing."

The constable's reply sent a pang through Waller, and brought him down to zero.

" But you haven't been out on the roof ? "

" No," said the sergeant mockingly, " nor we haven't been up the chimney. My lads are neither sweeps nor tilers. Think he's flown up there ? "

" No," said the constable with asperity ; " but I think you haven't half searched. Maybe he's hiding somewhere up in the ivy,"

" Ho ! " said the sergeant sharply. " Like a cock-sparrow or a rat, eh ? I tell you I have searched the place, and I have done."

" And I tell you you haven't half searched," cried the constable. " You must get ladders and go all over the roof. I daresay he's hiding in the ivy."

" Beg pardon, sergeant," said one of the men. " Didn't the good gentleman say something about some lunch ? "

" To be sure I did," said Waller, " and it will be ready in the kitchen by now."

" Thank you, sir," said the sergeant grumpily. " I suppose we shall be obliged to have a look at the roof from outside. I don't want to be reported to my captain for not having done my duty. But look here, Mr. Constable," and to Waller's great relief the man turned his back upon him and faced Gusset, while the boy felt as if he was turning white, and his hands grew moist. " You gave information," continued the sergeant, " and it seems to me that this is more your job than mine. How are we to get up on the roof ? "

" Ladder, of course," cried Gusset eagerly. " They have got long ones here that they use for the apples and stacks. You must get up out at the back."

" Oh, oh, oh ! " groaned Waller to himself. " I should like to have you out at the back ! "

" Oh, very well," said the sergeant. " Out with you, my lads, and let's get it over," and, as the men marched out, following the constable, who seemed quite at home in the geography of the house, the sergeant stopped to speak to Waller.

" There, sir, you see I can't help myself, so don't blame me."

" No," said Waller ; and, in spite of his efforts, his voice sounded very strange. But the man had turned away, and did not heed.

Gusset led the way into the big, open yard at the back, and, acting under his directions, the soldiers followed to a low shed, beneath which one of the long, thin, tapering ladders with straddling legs, used in country places, hung upon two great iron pegs against the wall.

" There you are," said Gusset. " Bring it out ! Quick ! "

" Here, I say," snarled one of the men he addressed, " who are you ordering about ? You are not our sergeant."

" There, don't talk, my lads," cried that individual, coming up. " Bring the ladder out and heave it up against that side of the house where the roof slopes."

At that moment the gardener, who had, as it were, been taken by surprise, and in the rear, came hurrying round from where he had been waiting by the porch in a great state of excitement.

" Here, I say ! Hold hard there ! " he cried. " What are you doing with my ladder ? Let it be ! I don't want that broke."

He turned to Waller as if to ask him to put a stop to it, but the boy avoided his gaze, thrust his hands deeply into his pockets, and stood frowning.

" Here, don't you interfere, Joe Hanson ; you will be getting yourself into trouble," spluttered Gusset, in his husky voice ; and he unconsciously blew out his cheeks and opened his eyes wider as he took a fresh

breath.   " This   here's   all   in   the   King's
name."

" King's name ! " cried the gardener sharply
as he lifted his blue serge apron and began to
twist it up in a tail to tuck up round his
waist.   " What's the King's name got to do
with it ?   I am talking about my ladder."

" There, there, gardener," said the sergeant, " don't stop us. I want to get this
job done. My boys don't understand ladders
like you do ; perhaps you wouldn't mind
pitching it up against the roof ? "

" Oh, very well, sergeant," replied the
gardener ; " I don't mind when I am asked
civilly, but I am not going to have all the
country cobblers in Hampshire coming into
my yard and meddling with the tools as is
in my charge. Here, that's not the way,
swaddy," he continued, joining the two
soldiers, who, each still holding his musket
in his hand, were fumbling awkwardly with
the long ladder in carrying it across the yard.

He smiled good-humouredly at the two
stiff-strapped and buckled-up men, and took
hold of the ladder about the middle.

" There, drop its heel on the ground," he
said, " and one of you put your foot on the
bottom round."

The soldier promptly obeyed, and the next minute, as the straddling bottom of the ladder was kept down, the gardener ran his hands along beneath it, thrusting it upward round by round till it was perpendicular, when, grasping it firmly, one hand low down and arms outstretched to the fullest extent, he walked quickly across the yard, planted the ladder down close to the house, and let the top fall away from him with a gentle *whish* amongst the ivy.

" Well done ! " cried the two soldiers admiringly ; and the gardener came away smiling with self-satisfaction at the men's admiration of his skill.

" Oh," he said to the sergeant, " it's easy enough when you know how."

" That's so, my lad," said the sergeant. " There's nothing like having a man who understands his tools."

Waller still stood frowning and rattling his knife, the key, a piece of curb chain, and a few other odds and ends in the bottom of his pocket, furtively watching the fat constable the while, till he caught sight of the sergeant looking at him, ready to half close his eye in a knowing wink.

" That'll about do," said Gusset ; and he

looked up to the top of the ladder, half hidden amongst the clustering ivy, then down at the two men, and, lastly, at the sergeant.

" Now, then," he said, in his unpleasant, husky voice, " it's no use to waste time. Somebody had better go up."

CHAPTER XVII.

A HOT SCENT.

" To be sure," said the sergeant sharply. " Well, we are waiting. You know the way better than we do. Up you go."

The constable turned upon him in astonishment, blowing out his cheeks and seeming to make his eyes roll, while his naturally rotund figure began more and more to assume the appearance of a fat cork float.

" Me ! Me ! Me go up there ! "

" To be sure," said the sergeant. " You country chaps are used to this sort of thing. My lads are not. Scaling ladders is more in our way, and they are bad enough when you have got to carry your Brown Bess."

" To be sure," said the gardener, chiming in, with a grin of satisfaction. " That's right enough, sergeant. Up you go, Fatty ! "

" You will get yourself into trouble, Joe Hanson," said the constable pompously. " This here's the second time I have warned you. You, sergeant—you know I can't get up there at my time of life, and it's your duty to send your men. I order you, in the King's name, to search that roof."

" Oh, very well," said the sergeant gruffly. " Here, number one and two, stand your muskets up against the wall. No, one of you only. You, Jem Cogan ; you are a light one. Up you go. You are not quite so heavy as the constable here."

" Haw ! haw ! haw ! " laughed the gardener. " That's a good one ! " And he bent down to slap his knees, while, to the constable's great disgust, the hoarse laugh was echoed in the shape of a titter uttered by the two maids, who had come to the back kitchen door.

Gusset blew out his cheeks again, and moved slowly towards the foot of the ladder, where, as the soldier placed his musket against the sill of one of the lower windows and then began lightly to ascend, Gusset set his feet very far apart, as if in imitation of the ladder, planted his fat hands upon his hips, and began to follow the private's movements, leaning somewhat back the while.

All at once there was a quick movement in the little group round the foot of the ladder, for, partly moved by the spirit of mischief, as well as by the intense desire to create a diversion, Waller made a rush.

" Hold hard a minute, soldier ! " he shouted " I know the way best ; let me come first."

As he spoke he literally charged at the constable, who was now leaning backwards a little out of his perpendicular, and came heavily in contact with him, forcing the man to make a snatch at one of the rounds to save himself from falling.

The next moment the top of the ladder began to glide sideways, describing an arc as it rustled through the ivy. The mounting soldier, feeling it go, made a jump to alight upon his feet, but, not having time to properly judge his distance, he came down upon the constable instead, and there followed a short scuffle, out of which Waller was the first to gain his feet, to turn savagely upon the heavy, sitting man, and exclaim, amidst roars of laughter :

" Why did you do that ? "

" Yes, "shouted the gardener ; " I saw him pull it over. Just look here, Master Waller ! Here's my beautiful new ladder snapped in two ! "

It was a fact. There lay the pieces ; and the soldier, whose face had flushed with rage, but who was not hurt, now joined in the laughter of those around, while the constable still sat looking piteously about, as if for the sympathy that did not come.

The sergeant was the next to speak; as he bent over and held out his hand.

" Well, you have done it now, master," he said. " I shouldn't have thought an old chap like you would get playing a trick like that."

" Oh ! " groaned Gusset, looking at him piteously. " Help me, please ! I think there's something broke ! "

" Not there," said the sergeant cheerily. " You wouldn't break ; you are too soft and inji-rubbery, old chap. Here, you two, set him on his pins again. I am very sorry. Mr. Froy, sir, about this ladder, but you see it wasn't my men's fault."

" No, of course not," said Waller. " They couldn't help it. Blundering up against the ladder like that ! It looks as if he had been drinking."

Meanwhile Gusset was " set upon his pins," again, as the sergeant expressed it—in other words, he was helped up, groaning and breathing hard, to look from one to the other for commiseration, but finding none.

" Well, this is all waste of time, my lads,"
said the sergeant, pulling himself together.
" I say, gardener, we must have another long
ladder, I suppose."

" You'll get no more of my ladders to
break," said the gardener, wagging his head,
" in the King's name or out of the King's
name."

" What ! " cried the sergeant, with mock
fierceness.

" Well, how can you," said the gardener,
" when there aren't none ? There's two
little ones as you can tie together if you like,
and Mrs. Gusset will lend you a bit of clothes-
line. But you wouldn't catch me venturing
my carkidge up them if she did. But you
can do as you like, unless old Waxy Fat would
like another try."

" The lunch is quite ready, Mr. Sergeant,"
came from the kitchen door at that moment.

" Thank you, ma'am," said the sergeant,
with a salute and a smile. Then he turned
and looked at the broken ladder, next at
Waller, and then at the mournful face of the
constable, who looked back at him in despair.

" Well, master," he said, " my lads aren't
much of angels, and they can't fly up on to
the roof, but they are looking hungry, as

fellows as haven't had a bite for the last six hours ; so, with your leave, Mr. Froy, sir, I will give orders for a flank attack upon that there bread and cheese.—Fall in, my lads ! Left face !   Forward ! March ! " and, placing himself by the leading file, he led the way straight up to the kitchen door, halted his men, gave the order to pile arms, and marched them into the kitchen, going himself directly after to collect his sentries and bring them up to the attack.

CHAPTER XVIII.

THE SEARCH RELINQUISHED.

THE little military party had no cause to complain of the hospitality of Brackendene.

The constable had, for, after staying behind, looking about him for sympathy, and finding none, the sound of the voices in the kitchen and the rattle of knives upon plates had such a strange effect upon him that it was quite curative, and, forgetting his injuries, he moved pompously up towards the kitchen door, feeling that, as one of the search-party, he had a right to partake of the refreshments.

But to his intense disgust he was met at the threshold by his plump, pleasant-looking sister, who planted herself, arms akimbo, right in his way.

" Well ? " she said sharply, and with an attempt to look fierce—which was a perfect failure, by the way, for Martha Gusset's was one of those countenances that never can by any possibility look angry, only a little comic when temper had the sway.

" No, not well, Martha," said the constable plaintively ; " but I don't think I am very much hurt."

" Serve you right if you were," said the cook, " coming here like this when master's out, and making a fuss about hidden spies, just to make people believe what a great person you are ! They don't know you like I do. Well, what do you want ? "

" The young Squire said we were all to have lunch, and I have dragged myself here to have mine."

" Dragged ? Rolled, you mean ! " cried his sister. " You grow more and more like a tub every day."

" But tubs have to be filled, Martha, dear," said the constable, with an attempt at a smile.

" Not in my kitchen if they do," said Martha, with a snort ; " and Master Waller never meant *you* to come in with the soldiers, so the sooner you go off back to the cottage the pleasanter it will be for you, for if I am put out I speak my mind, and I'm put out now so there ! "

Martha whisked herself round and marched back into the kitchen, while the constable, who seemed to have the yard to himself,

sighed, and went across to the mounting-
stone by the stable door, where he seated
himself to wait, intently watching the ivy-
clothed, highly pitched roof the while, till
one of the yard dogs came up cautiously
and slowly, and smelt him all round, but
made no further advance towards being
friends.

That lunch was rather prolonged, and, as
he listened, Waller, with his hands in his
pockets, marched up and down the hall,
frowning and thinking till he recalled the
breaking of the ladder and the aspect of the
village constable, when his frown faded away
as if by magic, and, throwing himself into one
of the big old oak hall chairs, he rolled about
in it, laughing silently till he cried.

At last a sharp order rang out in the kitchen,
and though he could not see, Waller heard the
men spring to their feet and march out into
the yard, where he followed quickly, in time
to see them take their piled muskets, while
Joe Hanson, the gardener, who had been playing his part at the lunch with greater zeal
than he bestowed upon his mowing or digging,
busied himself with picking up the broken
ladder, grinning across at Tony Gusset the
while.

Directly after there were a few parting words passing between Waller and the sergeant, the men joining in giving their young host a cheer, which struck very emptily upon Gusset's ear, and made him mutter vows about being even some day, as he scuffled across to get close up to the soldiers and march with them back to the village.

And now that all danger seemed to be over, Waller's spirits rose, and, in company with the gardener, he walked with the search-party along the drive, out at the gate, and along the road to the edge of the Squire's estate, keeping up a running fire the while to harass the rear of the column, which was formed by Tony Gusset, the actual rearguard being composed of the sergeant, who fell back with the pair from the Manor to march along silently and solemnly, though thoroughly enjoying the impromptu fun.

The gardener commenced it by calling out in an excited tone, as if he had suddenly recalled something :

" Here, hi ! Gusset ! "

" Yes," said the man, stopping, to turn round his great full-moon face.

" Why, you didn't take the soldiers to look at the cucumber-frames. Bound to say there's one of them there spies lying snug under the leaves."

" Ugh ! " grunted the constable angrily ; and he turned again and went on.

" I say, don't be in such a hurry ; there's the sea-kale pots, too."

" Ah, to be sure ! " cried Waller, loud enough for the constable to hear. " Gusset must be right. Better come back and have another look. He may be in one of the sties disguised as a pig."

Just then the road was leading them along by the bank of a fine old hammer pond, a great black-looking pool surrounded by a dense growth of alders and water-loving shrubs, while sedge, reed, and rush flourished wonderfully, and formed a mazy home for the abundant moorhens and coots.

As the party moved onward to the village there was a sudden rush and a splash, and Waller called upon the sergeant to stop.

" Here's a likely place, sergeant," he said.

" Nonsense ! " said the man, " I know what that splash was. It was a big pike."

" It might have been," said the gardener, grinning, " but it's more like the sort of splash a French spy would make when he saw soldiers' scarlet jackets. Why don't you make old Waxy dive in and have a hunt all round under the bushes ? "

" No, don't, sergeant," put in Waller. " It's ten feet deep in some places."

" Pooh ! What does that matter ? " cried the gardener, who, like the boy, spoke loud enough for the constable to hear. " He wouldn't mind. He'd sink to the bottom and walk about safely all over the mud."

" That he wouldn't," cried Waller. " He'd shoot up to the top again like a cork."

And then the banter ceased, for the sergeant's men passed through the swing gate, and to Waller's great relief he was able to make his way back to the hall, very silent now as he went over the day's proceedings, and thought of the chances of the men coming back to make a fresh search, while the gardener kept on harping metaphorically upon the broken ladder, and what " master would say " when he came back.

At last the boy got rid of him, and made his way into the house, where he had a hard fight to curb his inclinations to rush up at once to his room.

This desire he kept down till he had made

sure that the servants were at their dinner, and then, after a cautious saunter about the grounds to convince himself that the gardener had gone to his cottage, Waller hurried up, and paused breathlessly at the door of his den, which he opened and closed, and then locked himself in.

The next minute he had crept out of the window, to hold on by the sill and feel with his feet amongst the ivy for the stone gutter which ran all along the front of the house. Upon this, half hidden by the ivy, he proceeded cautiously to his right, where a deep gully between two gables went right across the house, with the ivy positively rioting and pretty well filling it up with long strands and great berry-bearing clumps. Here, completely hidden, Waller crept along three or four yards.

" Only me," he said merrily. " Don't shoot ! How are you getting on ? "

A head and shoulders were slowly raised from among the thick glossy leaves, and he was confronted by Godfrey's sombre countenance.

" Miserably," he said. " I had hoped that this despicable hiding was at an end. Pray help me to-night to get away."

" Oh, I know what's the matter with you,"
cried Waller. " You are hungry and tired
out.   But come along back into my room.
But I say, you found it easy enough to get
here, didn't you ?   I was in a fright at first ;
then I thought that you would be sure to
creep out."

" Oh, yes, easy enough," said the lad.   " Is
the enemy quite gone ? "

" Yes, right away, and well satisfied. They
won't come again."

" Why do you speak like that ? " said
Godfrey, sharply.   " It sounded as if you were
afraid that somebody else would come."

" Well," said Waller slowly, " I am not
quite satisfied about our fat-headed constable.
He's very suspicious, and wanted to search
the roof. But I managed to put a stop to
that, for if they had got up here you must have
been found."

" Yes," said Godfrey, as, after following
his companion back through the ivy, he
seated himself, away from the window, in the
den, where Waller related to him the history
of the raising of the ladder.

" That man believes I am here, and will
come again. It is quite time you got me away.
It was he who came prowling round the house

last night, and not your gardener—a big, heavy man, not like Hanson at all."

" Yes, you are right," said Waller ; " and he must have seen you in the lane and gone and sought out the soldiers at once."

CHAPTER XIX.

PLANS OF ESCAPE.

THE days glided on and there was no news of the Squire's coming back, and no fresh alarm or suggestion of the possibility of the soldiers returning to make another search, so Waller grew more and more satisfied in the belief that, however much Gusset might suspect, it was merely suspicion, and there was no more to fear.

"I think at any time now we might begin to think of making a start." said Waller one morning.

"Yes, yes," cried Godfrey eagerly.

"Well, you needn't look so pleased because you are going," cried Waller, half angrily, but dropping his voice directly lest it should be heard and let the servants know he had somebody up there to whom he was talking.

"Oh, don't speak to me like that," crie d Godfrey earnestly. "I don't want to go but I am afraid it would be bad for both of us, and lead to trouble if I stayed."

"Well, I suppose so," said Waller. "As

I say, I don't want you to go, but it will be better for both of us when you are on your way back to France."

The boy stopped speaking and stood looking earnestly in his companion's eyes, while Godfrey shook his head and then held out his hand.

Waller was about to take it, feeling very miserable the while, for he was growing very much attached to his nervous, excitable companion, when both started violently, for some one had come up in perfect silence and given a sharp tap or two at the door.

In the full conviction that whoever it was must have heard the talking, Waller caught up the hammer near at hand, then threw it down noisily upon his work-bench, and walked quickly to the door.

" What is it ? " he cried.

The answer came in Bella's voice :

" You are wanted, Master Waller."

" Who wants me ? " said Waller, changing colour and seeing all sorts of imaginary dangers below.

" Don't know, sir. Martha told me to come and tell you somebody's there. I think it's the soldiers come again."

Waller compressed his lips, and could not have spoken for a few moments if it had been to save his life, while he gazed despairingly at his companion.

" Say I will come down directly," he almost gasped, and to divert the maid's attention, he hammered sharply on his work-bench, gazing dejectedly at his companion the while, as they both listened to the girl's descending footsteps.

" Don't be downhearted," he whispered. " It may mean nothing. I'll lock you in and go down. If anything does go wrong and you hear people coming up, make for the hiding place in the ivy again. And look here, I don't believe they will find where you are hidden, but take the coil with you, and if anyone is coming to search the roof, make the rope fast to one of the chimney-stacks, watch for your chance, slide down, and then make for the forest to find a hiding-place somewhere down by the river."

" And what then ? You'll never find me."

" Oh, yes, I will, and if you hear three little twits like a blackbird's, only louder, you can answer, for it will be I."

There was no time for more, so Waller

slipped out and went down, expecting to see the redcoats in the hall; but there was no one there, and he went on into the kitchen.

" Who wants me, cook ? " he said.

" It's that Bunny Wrigg, Master Waller, come begging, I suppose, because he knows master's out."

With a sigh of relief and the wish at his heart that he could send Godfrey the news at once that there was nothing to fear, the boy went out into the yard, where the big, brown, gipsy-like ne'er-do-well of the place was holding a fine freshly washed turnip in one hand, his knife in the other, busily munching a slice.

" Oh, it's you, Bunny, is it ? "

" Yes, Master Waller ; me it is."

" Where did you get that turnip ? "

" Joe Hanson giv'it me, sir. It's one of yours, and it's prime."

" Joe has no business to give things away when father's out—not to anybody."

" Oh, I aren't anybody, Master Waller," said the man, with a grin. " I'm nobody, and don't count."

" Well, look here ; I don't want to know anything about any strange birds or polecats or owls or hawks or anything. I am busy now. There's a shilling for you. Be off."

" You're busy, are you ? "

" Yes, very."

" Hah ! Shilling, eh ? I don't want it."

" First time I ever knew you refuse money."

" Ah, but that's only a shilling. I want a lot."

" Well, of all the impudence ! I shan't give you any more, so toddle."

" Nobody asked you—I say, I know ! "

" Know what ? "

" About the hundred pounds "

" What hundred pounds ? " said Waller, starting.

" What you are going to get for ketching that chap," said the man, with a grin.

" Catching what chap ? " cried Waller sharply.

" Ah, you know. Why, I always sleep with my eyes open. It's a hundred pounds for ketching that spy, as they calls him ; and as he was caught in my woods I say halves."

" You don't know what you are talking about," cried Waller fiercely, blustering to hide the faint qualm he felt. " Spy ! Hundred pounds ! Halves ! Here, you had better be off before you get into a row. Your woods, indeed ! What next ? "

" I d'know, and don't want to. All I know is that they are wild, and as much mine as anybody else's. Now then, what about them halves ? "

" Look here, Bunny ; what have you got in your head ? "

" Hidees, Master Waller. Never you mind what I have got in my head ; it's what have you got up in your room where you are always cobbling and tinkering and making things ? "

" Bunny ! " cried Waller, staggered for the moment out of his assurance.

" Yes ; that's me, Master Waller, and I want fifty pound. Lot of money, ar'n't it ? And I want money. You are a rich gentle-man, and don't, and ought to give me the whole hundred. But I don't want to be grasping, because it's you, and so I says halves."

" But, Bunny——" cried Waller.

" Oh, it ar'nt no use for you to talk. I know all about it, and the soldiers coming to sarch and then going away because they couldn't find nothing, when you had got him hid away all the time."

" Oh, Bunny ! " cried Waller huskily.

" That's me. I tell you I know, so it's no use to tell no taradiddlums about it. I see you taking him out for a walk last night to stretch his legs."

Waller's eyes fixed in a stare, and his lips parted as he breathed harder than usual.

" You see, I'm about arter dark when other folks goes to sleep. I come and had a look at him t'other night when you thought everybody was a-bed."

" You coward ! " said Waller, in a hoarse whisper, and his hands opened and shut as he felt ready to spring at the man's throat.

" That I warn't. Man ar'n't no coward who swarms up that there ivy, which as like as not will break away, being as brittle as carrots."

" You came to look in and spy ? " half whispered Waller.

" That I didn't. I ar'n't the spy ; it's 'im. I swarmed up the ivy to see if that there young ullet was fit to take. But it warn't. But I seed you'd got a light up there, so I went along sidewise, till I could look in. There was you two, laughing and talking together in whispers, and after a bit you jumps up and come and opened the window."

"Ah!" gasped Waller. "But you weren't there?"

"I warn't there! Warn't I just? Why, the window scraped over my head and knocked my cap off as I bobbed down. There, it's no use for you to pretend, Master Waller, so just you hand over that there fifty pounds."

Waller was silent for a few moments, and his eyes wandered in all directions save that where the rough-looking woodman stood. At last, after drawing a deep breath, he said in a hoarse whisper :

"Come along this way."

"Wheer to, lad?"

"Out in the woods."

"Ar'n't a-going to try and do for me so as to keep all the hundred pounds yourself, are you, Master Waller?" said the rough fellow, with a grin.

"No, of course not. I want to talk to you."

"That's right, lad. I wouldn't try to do t'other, because you might get hurt, and I shouldn't like to hurt you, Master Waller, because you have been a good friend to me, and I like you, lad, and I'm waiting to see you grow up into being the finest gentleman in

these parts. You won't never want to chivy
me out of the woods, I know."

Waller uttered a low hiss, and hurried on in
silence till they stood together among the
nut stubs overshadowed by the spreading oaks,
when he stopped short and faced round.

" You say you know that I shall never
chivy you out of the woods, Bunny ; but
you know wrong, for I should like to do it
now."

" Get out, lad !   Not you !   Why ? "

" For being such a coward and sneak, and
coming here to gather blackmail and betray
that poor fellow to the gallows, or to be
shot."

" What are you talking about, lad ?   What
if he is put away ?   He's only a spy, come
here to do harm to the King."

" That's nothing to do with you," cried
Waller.

" Nay, but the money is.   Half a hundred
pounds is a lot.   You needn't make a fuss ;
you'll get your share.   What's he to you ?
Has he broke his leg, same as I did mine,
when I wouldn't go away into the workus,
and you used to come and see me and talk
to me till it got better ? "

" Broken his leg ?   No ! "

" Ho !   Thought he had perhaps, because you like doctoring chaps as has broke their legs, as well I know.   What is he to you, then, Master Waller ? "

" He's my friend, Bunny," cried the boy passionately.   " One I'd do anything to save from harm ;   one I like as if he were my brother.   And here you come, after all the kindness that I have shown you, and want to do me the greatest harm that man could do."

" That I don't."

" What !   Why, you come here threatening to go and betray that poor fellow to the soldiers if I don't give you fifty pounds."

" That I didn't, Master Waller.   I want for you and me to go and give him up fair and square, and take the money, before someone else does."

" What ! " cried Waller, catching him by the arm.   " Somebody else ?   Does anyone but you know he's there ? "

" Like enough, lad," said the man, with a grin.

" But you haven't betrayed him ? "

" Not likely, lad.   I say to myself, I says, ' If anybody is going to get that money it's Master Waller and me, not old Fatty Gusset, who brought the soldiers up t'other day.' "

" But he doesn't believe he's here now,
does he, Bunny ? "

" Shouldn't wonder if he does, Master
Waller.   He ar'n't so stupid as he looks. He's
as cunning as he is fat.   A lot of the fox in
him.   It's you as ought to have the money,
seeing that it was only right when you found
him, and have fed the Frenchy beggar ever
since."

" But who else is likely to know ? "

" Haw !   Haw ! " laughed the man, shak-
ing with pure enjoyment at what seemed to
him one of the greatest jokes in the world.
" You have never seen him.   You ar'n't got
him chained up to your work-bench up in
your room !   Oh, no !   But I say, Master
Waller, you can fib when you like ! "

" How dare you ! " cried Waller angrily.
" How have I fibbed or lied to you ?   Didn't
I own it to you directly, sir, as soon as I was
sure you knew ? "

" Oh, well, I suppose you did, Master
Waller.   Beg pardon !   Don't be waxy with
me, lad."

" Here, tell me who is likely to know."

" Why, Joe Hanson, like as anybody, I
should say.   If I had bin him I know I should
soon have had the forty-round apple ladder

up agen your window to see what you were about."

" Anyone else ? " cried Waller.

" Ay. Old Fatty Gusset, as aforesaid ; old cobbler ! "

" But you haven't dropped a hint, Bunny ?"

" Dropped a hint ! Na—ay ! I'd sooner drop his old lapstone on his toe."

" Look here, Bunny ! " cried Waller, catching the man by the wrist, while an inquisitive-looking robin hopped nearer to them from twig to twig, and sat watching them both with its bright, bead-like eyes.

" Look wheer, my lad ? "

" Look here ! You don't want fifty pounds."

" Oh, don't I ! Hark at him ! " cried the man, laughing. and addressing the robin.

" Why, what good would it be to you ? "

" What good, lad ? Why, I'd have a noo thick weskit, a plush un, before the winter come—a red un like his'n," and he nodded towards the robin.

" Bah ! Nonsense ! "

" Nay, it ar'n't, lad. Them red uns are strange and warm, and lies down like feathers. Then there's boots. I'd like a pair of the stoutest and thickest lace-up waterproofers as I could get—not a pair of old Fatty's cobbling, but real down good uns, out of Southampton's town."

" Yes ! " panted Waller, " And what else would you do with the money ? "

" Waal, I don't know about what else," said the man thoughtfully. " That there weskit and them boots would about do for the present."

" That wouldn't cost two pounds," cried Waller ; " and what would you do with the other ? "

" Bury it in an old pot." said the man, with a grin. " I know a hole as would take that."

" Oh, Bunny ! " cried the boy passionately, " I thought better of you ! I did think you were a man ! "

" So I am," cried the fellow fiercely. " Who says I ar'n't ? "

" I do ! " cried Waller, dashing his arm away. " For the sake of a warm waistcoat and a pair of stout boots you would give up that poor fellow to be hanged, or see him shot ! "

" Not me, lad ! " cried Bunny fiercely.

" You would, sir ! Why, I'd sooner go shivering and barefoot all my days than even think of such a thing."

" Phe—ew ! " growled the man, and he began scratching the thick, dark curls, almost negro-like, that covered his head and hung over his broad brown temples. " Why, I never thought anything like that, Master Waller. Why, I would'nt go and see a man shot nor hung for love or money ! I only thought about that chap as being a spy as had come here to steal the crown ; and it seemed to me, as you found him, that it'd be about fair if you and me went snacks with the reward. Look here, my lad, I'll get my old weskit covered with a bit of heifer-skin, and as for the boots, why, they'll do for another winter yet if I lay 'em up pretty thick with grease. Don't you get waxy with me, Master Waller. I didn't mean no harm. I wouldn't hurt that poor chap, especially as you like him."

" No, Bunny," cried the boy, catching his arm again. " I'm sure you wouldn't ; and you won't tell upon me ? "

" You say I ar'n't to, Master Waller, and, of course, I won't."

" Then I do say you are not to. I wouldn't have that poor fellow found and taken for the world."

" All right, Master Waller."

" And as for the money you will miss,

Bunny, I have got some saved up, and you shall have the waistcoat and the boots before a month's passed."

" Na—ay, I shan't," growled the man. " Bang the boots and the weskit ! I won't have 'em now. You say it's right for that there poor young chap to be took care of, and it shall be done. You have got him all right up there ; but your father's coming home. What will he say ? "

" Oh, don't talk about it," cried the boy excitedly. " It makes me shiver ! "

" Do it ? Well, look here, lad ; when you know he's coming home, you hand the chap over to me."

" What, could you hide him somewhere ? "

" Could I hide him somewhere ? Haw ! Haw ! " laughed the man. " He says, could I hide him somewhere ? " And he looked round as if to address the robin ; but the bird had flitted away, and Bunny Wrigg gazed straight in the boy's eyes again. " Of course I could, lad, and where no soldiers could find him and even you couldn't. You let me have him, and he'll be all right."

" Bunny, you are a good fellow ! " cried Waller excitedly. " And you shall have the best waistcoat and boots that money can buy."

"Nay I sha'n't, lad," growled the man, "and if you say any more about them things I shan't play. That there young Frenchy chap must be a good sort, or you wouldn't have made him your friend. Why, I'd rather hear you call me a good fellow like you did just now, and think of me, being the young Squire, as your friend, than have all the weskits in the world. But I say, look here, Master Waller," said Bunny thoughtfully, "I could hide that chap in one of my snuggeries; but what about the winter time?"

"What about the winter time?" said Waller, staring.

"Ay; when it's always raining, or snow's on the ground. I don't mind, because the water runs off me, same as it would off a wild duck; and as for the frost and snow, I could roll in 'em like a dog. But such a chap as your friend—it'd kill him in no time. He'd be catching colds and sore gullets, and having the roomis."

"Oh, but it wouldn't be for long."

"What are you going to do with him then? Not setting anybody else to take care of him?"

"Oh, no, no, Bunny."

" Because I shouldn't like that, sir, when I'd undertook the job. What are you going to do with him then ? "

" Wait till the soldiers are gone, Bunny, and then get him down to the coast and smuggle him aboard a fishing-boat and get the skipper to run him across to Cherbourg or St. Malo."

" Ho ! " said Bunny, thoughtfully, and then, giving his thigh a slap, " They wouldn't do it, sir. I mean the skipper wouldn't."

" Wouldn't do it ? " cried Waller.

" Not him, sir. Why, he'd want five shillings at least before he'd stir."

" Five shillings ! " cried Waller contemptuously. " Why, Bunny, I'd give him five pounds."

" You would, sir ? Then hooroar ! "

" What do you mean by your hooroar ? " cried Waller.

" Why, hooroar, of course, I've got the chap as would do it."

" Where ? " cried Waller.

" Why, I ar'n't got him in my pocket, lad, but there's my brother-in-law, him and his two mates, who've got a lugger of their own. Down yonder by Loo Creek, facing the Isle, you know. Five pounds ! Why, they have to go and lay out their nets a many times to get five pounds. They'd do it—leastways, brother-in-law Jem would. Cherbourg, eh ? Why, he's been there lots of times."

" Splendid, Bunny ? " cried Waller eagerly ; and then, looking solemn at the thought of parting from his new friend : " But could you trust him, Bunny ? "

" Trust him, sir ? "

" Yes. I mean, he wouldn't betray the poor fellow, would he ? "

Bunny stared at Waller for a moment, and then moistened both his hands, gave them a rub together, and clenched them.

" He'd better ! " he said. " Why, I'd— I'd—I'd—half smash him ! Nay, I wouldn't —I'd take his wife away. Sister Jen wouldn't stop along with a sneak. But bah ! Fisherman Jem ! You might trust him anywhere. He'd want stirring up to make him go, but me and the five pounds would make that all right."

" Oh, I oughtn't to have doubted him, Bunny ; he's your brother-in-law ; that's enough for me. Then, as soon as the soldiers are gone—I don't want to, and I suppose I oughtn't to—but we will get him down to the lugger and send him off home to come to his senses."

" Ah ! " cried Bunny, " and you tell him, Master Waller, to stop there, for it ar'n't honest to come here trying to steal the King's crown."

" No," said Waller, laughing ; " of course not, Bunny. Now, look here, you keep a sharp look-out without seeming to be watching the soldiers and Tony Gusset, and if there's anything wrong you come and tell me."

" Right, Master Waller ! That's so ; and look here, sir. When we get him down to the creek and take him aboard he'd better be dressed up a bit so as people shan't take no notice of him. You make him put on some of your oldest clothes, and keep him three or four days wi'out weshing his hands and face. That'll make him look more nat'ral."

" Oh, we'll see about that, Bunny ; and now you do this. You go down to Loo Creek and see your brother-in-law at once. But look here ; you'll want some money."

" What for ? " said the man sharply.

" Oh, to pay somebody for giving you a lift, and for something to eat, because you won't be able to do it all in a day."

" Oh, you let me alone for that."

" I shan't," said Waller. " Here, take this."

" I shan't neither," said the man, and he made a little resistance, which ended in Waller thrusting a couple of half-crowns into his pockets. " Say, Master Waller, you and me has had some games in these 'ere woods in our time, ar'n't us ? "

" Yes, Bunny ! Hundreds."

" But this 'ere's quite a new un, eh ? "

" New indeed, Bunny."

" Ay, and I'm beginning to like it, too, lad. Well, I suppose I must be off."

" But, Bunny, may I depend on you that you will keep this a secret ? "

" May you depend on me, lad ? Why, ar'n't I said it ? Did yer ever know me not keep my word ? "

" Never ! " cried Waller.

" Then look 'ere, sir. That means mum."

" That " was a smart slap on the mouth, Bunny's metaphorical way of showing that the secret of the young enthusiast who had come, as he believed, to fight for and rescue a lost cause, was within that casket and he had banged down the lid.

CHAPTER XX.

"WHAT are you thinking about?" said Waller.

" Thinking," replied Godfrey.

" Yes ; you haven't spoken a word for the last five minutes."

The two lads were standing together with their elbows resting on the sill of the wide dormer window, whose two casements were propped wide open, while they gazed out into the soft darkness of the autumn night.

" I was thinking about that friend of yours who was going to get me a pass across to France in a fishing-boat."

" Oh," said Waller in a disappointed tone ; " I thought you were thinking about how beautiful it is looking out here into the darkness of the forest, with the scent of the soft, warm, damp leaves, and listening to the owls and that squeaking rabbit that had the weasel after it."

" It is very beautiful," said Godfrey sadly ; " but I was thinking about that boat."

" I wish you wouldn't be so fond of wishing

to get away," said Waller gloomily. " It's as if I had not done enough to make you comfortable."

" Oh ! " cried the lad passionately, and he turned to lay his hand on Waller's shoulder. " How can you say that, when you have done too much, and made me feel—almost alone in the world as I am—as if I should like to stay here always ! "

" Do you mean that ? " cried Waller excitedly.

" Of course I do. I never had a friend like you before, and I never knew what it was to lead a boy's life. Out there in France I never heard about anything else hardly but politics, and getting back the crown for the Stuarts."

" Then you really don't want to go ? " cried Waller.

" No ; but I must go, and the sooner the better. You know what I must feel."

" Yes," said Waller sadly, " but——"

" Oh, it must come to an end. I lie awake of a night wondering how it is that your servants have not found it all out before, with you bringing up all that I have to eat and drink. I fancy sometimes that they must know."

" But they don't," said Waller grimly.

" But how have you managed ? "

" Oh, somehow," said Waller, with a half-laugh. " It's been mostly done by stealing."

" By stealing ! Nonsense ! You couldn't be a thief."

" Thank you for the compliment," said Waller, laughing ; " but you are wrong. I have gone on stealing every day, everything you have had ; only it was only my own breakfast and dinner."

" Then you have been starving yourself for me ! " said Godfrey excitedly.

" Oh, no, I haven't," cried Waller merrily, " only I've got the credit of being such a pig that cook's quite anxious about me. It was only the day before yesterday she wanted me to take some physic ; said I was eating twice as much as was good for me, and it made her very anxious, and she wished my father would come home."

" Yes," cried Godfrey, " your father, too. Why, you told me long ago that you expected him every day."

" Well, so I did ; but he doesn't come, and he doesn't write. I don't know why it is ; but, of course, he will come some day."

" Yes, and there will be terrible trouble

about your harbouring me. Oh, Waller, I did hope your man of the woods would have got a passage for me in some boat. Why, it's four days since he was here and promised to make that right."

"Oh, give him time," said Waller impatiently; "and do pray leave off grumbling when things are going so well."

"Going so well?"

"Yes, I didn't tell you. I was saving it up, only we got talking about other things. I have some news. The soldiers are gone. I am sorry to say."

"You are sorry to say?"

"Why, of course," said Waller sadly. "Doesn't it mean that I have to keep my promise and help to get you away?"

"Yes," said Godfrey softly, and his fingers began to grip his companion's shoulder; "but some day I hope that I shall be able to cross over again, not as a poor fugitive, but in peace, and come here and see you, if you will have me when I am not a prisoner."

"If I will have you, lad!" cried Waller enthusiastically. "Why, you know I will; and my father will be glad to see you too, if you don't come, as old Bunny said, to try and steal the crown. Why, of course, you and I are going to be friends always. And you will write to me, and I shall write to you."

"Yes, yes; of course," cried Godfrey eagerly. "I don't want to go away, Waller, but I must; and as that man—Bunny you call him—does not bring us any news, I want you to let me start off to-morrow night as soon as it is dark, and make my way to Southampton."

"To be caught and put in prison," cried Waller, "and——Bother that owl! That's the third time it has hooted this last five minutes. No!" he cried in an excited whisper, as he rested his hands on the window-sill. "Hist! It's Bunny Wrigg!" And then, clapping his hands to each side of his mouth, he softly imitated with wonderful accuracy the call of one of the woodland owls.

"*Hoi hoi hoi hoi hoi!*"

"*Pee-week! Pee-week! Pee-week!*" came from below them in the shrubbery a little to their left.

"All right, Bunny," whispered Waller. "I'll come down."

"Nay, lad; hold hard. I'm coming up."

The darkness was so dense that, as the lads gazed down, they had but a mere glimpse of a shadowy animal, as it seemed to be running

across the lawn, and directly after there was
a faint, soft rustling in the thick ivy.

"Isn't it dangerous for him?" whispered
Godfrey.

"Not it. Bunny can climb like a cat.
He'll be right up in the big gutter directly."

The lad was quite correct, for, with wonderfully little noise, considering, the active
fellow climbed up by the huge old stems of the
ivy, and a couple of minutes later he was
standing in the stone gutter, holding on by
the division between the open casements.

"Catch hold of this 'ere bundle—on my
back," he whispered. "It's only hanging on
by the strap over my neck."

Waller did as he was told, and, pulling the
strap over the man's head, he drew a big soft
bundle into the room.

"That's your sort," whispered Bunny.
"If I tried to clamber in with that on it would
have ketched."

The next moment he was gliding in over the
window-sill, slowly and softly like a huge
black slug, and ended by seating himself
cross-legged on the floor.

"Anybody hear me if I talk?"

"No, but speak low," whispered Waller.
while Godfrey's breath was quite audible as

he breathed hard in his excitement. "We were beginning to think that you did not mean to come."

"What call had you got to think that?" grumbled the man in a hoarse whisper. "I went directly.—How are you, young gentleman?—My brother-in-law Jem had gone to sea, and I had to wait; and here I am now, large as life and twiced as ugly."

"But has your brother-in-law come back?"

"Oh, ay, he's got back."

"And will he take my friend across to Cherbourg?"

"Oh, I have been having a long fight with him about that, sir. He's got a nasty disposition, he has. I telled him that I'd give him a good price for doing the job, and that I'd go as far as three pounds."

"What!" cried Waller. "I told you five."

"To be sure you did, sir, but I warn't going to let him have all his own way, so I said three, meaning, if he argufied very much, to spring another pound and make it four. But he wouldn't. He stuck out for the five, and I had to promise him."

"Oh, but you shouldn't have wasted time over that, Bunny."

"Don't you tell me, Master Waller. I know brother Jem better than you do. He's a close-fisted one, brother Jem is, and he always takes care that them as buys his fish to sell ashore shan't have too much profit. Why, if I had offered him five pound right off he'd have held out for six. But don't you get wasting time talking. There aren't none to lose."

"No time to lose? What do you mean?" said Waller.

"Ah, you don't know, then? The soldiers is coming here to-night."

"To-night! Nonsense!" cried Waller. "They have gone right away—to Chichester, I think."

"Maybe they went, sir, but it warn't to Chichester; it was to Christchurch; and Tony Gusset got hold of something, and he's gone after them, and some one I know telled me they were coming here to-night, and don't mean to be put off this time."

"Then I must go at once," cried Godfrey excitedly.

"That's right, sir," said Bunny. "I brought you some things as will make you look like a fisher-lad when I have done with you. Can you slip them on in the dark?"

"Oh, yes, of course he can," cried Waller. "I will help him."

"The sooner the better, then, sir," whispered the man, and, busying himself with the knots in a great cotton handkerchief, he soon shook out a big, broad, canvas petticoat, such as the fishers use, sewed right up the middle so as to give it the semblance of a clumsy pair of trousers.

Godfrey winced a little as he handled the stiff garment ; but it was for liberty, and he soon had the canvas buttoned on.

"You had better take off that jacket, sir. I can't see it, but I can feel as it don't look a bit like a fisher-boy's things. That's your sort ! Now then, Master Waller, pull that there jersey over his head. That's the way. There, now, he feels like a regular sailor-lad. Here's a sou'-wester, too. It's rather an old un, but none the worse for that. There you are. Now then, I have got a bit of a pot here. You hold your hands, and I'll fish out a dob of it with my knife. Then you give it a good rub round with your hands so as to go all over them, and then you can gorm them well over your face. Don't be afraid of it, sir. It'll make you look every bit a sailor, and won't wash off in a month."

Godfrey drew in his breath with a hiss.

" Why, what is it, Bunny ? " said Waller.

" Real good pitch, sir, same as they pays over the bottoms of their boats."

" Oh, but surely that isn't necessary," cried Waller angrily.

" He's right," said Godfrey, as he began to rub the sticky brown produce of the fir well over his hands and face. " It's the best disguise I could assume."

" Hist ! " said Waller. " Didn't I hear something ? "

Bunny turned to the window, looked out cautiously, and drew in his head again.

" They've come," he whispered. " Now sir, can't you get us down to the back door, so that we can slip away at once ? "

" No," said Waller excitedly. " We should have to cross the hall, and they'd be there."

" I'm all right," said Bunny. " I can slip down easier than I got up. What about this here young gentleman ? He won't find it so easy with that there canvas on."

" No," cried Waller. " He couldn't get down. I don't believe I could. What in the world are we to do ? "

" Ar'n't got a bit of rope, I suppose, sir ? " whispered Bunny.

" Yes, of course. I'd forgotten."

" Strong un ? "

" The new one I got for the fishing-net,"
said Waller.

" That'll do it. Now then, let me look
out while you get it. You make it fast to
the big window-bar while I just try and see
what they are doing. I want to make sure
that they all go in and leave the way clear
for us to slide down. Once we can get to
the woods we shall be all right."

" Make sure," whispered Waller, " that
they don't leave a sentry by the porch."

Bunny grunted, and as silently as he could
Waller took his coil of rope from the drawer,
fastened it again to the beam, and, as soon as
the man drew in his head, prepared to lower
it down.

" It's all right, my lad. Be quick. Some
of them has gone round to the back, and your
gal Bella has just let t'others in by the front
door. Here, I'll go down first to see if the
rope's safe, and ready to knock over any of
them sojers if he tries to stop us. The young
gent had better come next, and you last.
You'll have to leave the rope to get back
after you have seen us a bit on the way. But
hold hard a minute. How long is that rope ?"

"About thirty yards," said Waller.

"Here, let me get at it," said Bunny, and, rapidly unfastening it, he ran it through his hands till he could put the two ends together to get its measurement, and then, passing an end on either side of the upright division of the window, he lowered it down till the bight came in contact with the upright bar. "There you are," he whispered; "twice as strong; and when we are all down I can haul on one end and bring it after us to hide it somewheres in the wood so as it shan't give you away."

"Capital!" whispered Waller, hurrying to the window, thrusting out his head, and listening, to find all still. "No one there," he whispered again, "so down with you."

Bunny gave a grunt, took hold of the rope, and as he was squeezing himself out to stand with his feet in the gutter. Waller caught hold of his friend's hand, gave it a grip, and then crept to the door, turned the key softly, opened it and listened there, to hear the murmur of voices down in the hall.

He turned the key again and darted back to the window, to feel the rope quivering for a few moments and then slacken.

Bunny was at the bottom.

" Now can I help you ? " whispered Waller.

" No," was the reply. " I can manage."
But Waller's heart beat fast and a strange
choking sensation seemed to rise in his breast
as the boy, hampered by his stiff petticoat-
trousers, had no little difficulty in getting
clear of the window.

The next minute he was letting himself
glide down, rustling loudly through the ivy.

Waller waited, leaning half out of the window and gazing down till he was satisfied that
his companion was nearly at the bottom,
when he hurried back to the door, unlocked
it and withdrew the key, and then, opening,
he felt for the hole and thrust the key in on
the outer side.

" There," he muttered ; " when they come
up here, they won't suspect me."

It was his turn now, and, full of activity,
he crept out of the window and stood for a
moment amongst the ivy in the gutter, and
then began to slide so quickly down the
double rope that his hands were ready to
burn. As he touched the soft earth he felt
Bunny thrust him aside and take hold of one
end of the rope.

" You haul steadily," he whispered ; and as
the lad drew on the rope the big country fellow

laid it in rings at his feet. "Mind your head,"
he whispered, "when t'other end falls."

But Waller was on his guard, and as the end
glided round the upright of the window-
frame and came rustling down through the
ivy, it just touched the lad's protecting arm,
and that was all.

"I'll hide this here somewhere, where I
can find it again," whispered Bunny. "You
won't want to go in again that way when
there's the doors."

As the last ring was formed of the rope
and caught up by the rough gipsy-looking
fellow, they stood listening to the sound of
voices, which came loudly from within, two
of those present recognising the husky, throaty
speech of the village constable, and Waller
set it down to questioning as to where he was.

Directly after, at a word from Bunny, they
stepped off the bed on to the soft turf, just
as there was the rattle of a lock, the big door
was thrown open, and a bright bar of light
flashed across the lawn, while *clump, clump,*
came the heavy footsteps of a couple of the
soldiers marching through the porch.

To go on seemed to Waller like courting
danger ; to stand still suggested the cer-
tainty of being seen ; and giving Godfrey a

thrust, he pressed onward, risking all, and following Bunny, who was hurrying in the direction of the forest.

Over and over again Waller felt certain that they must be seen by the two men, whom he could make out as he glanced back, standing against the light that came through the porch, and he could hardly believe in their good fortune, as neither shout nor shot was sent in their direction, while a few minutes later they were threading their way amongst the trees.

CHAPTER XXI.

THE ESCAPE.

" WELL, so far so good," said Bunny softly.
" We are not likely to meet anybody in the
hevenue, Master Waller, so that's the best
going, and we will keep to that."

" The soldiers will be all up at the Manor,
but suppose anybody else is coming up from
the village ? "

" If they was I should 'ear them, sir,
before they 'eard me. We will step out, and
when you think it best, Master Waller, you
turn back, and make yourself easy. I'll see
young squire here safe aboard brother Jem's
boat some time to-morrow, so you had better
say good-bye pretty sharp so as to be ready
to slip off when you like. But what about
that there money ? Shall I tell brother Jem
as I have it ready for him and his mates when
he's set young squire here safe across ? "

" Yes, of course," cried Waller.

" Pst ! " whispered the man. " In among
the trees ! " and he caught hold of Godfrey's
hand, dragging him through the bracken and

bush, while in his excitement Waller took cover on the other side of the winding way.

For all at once he was conscious of the flashing of two lights and the dull rattle of wheels coming through the deep sand of the road.

Directly after the lights were illumining the big trunks of the fine old trees through which the track ran, and the boy's heart beat all the faster as through the open window of the post-chaise he caught a glimpse of the grey, stern-looking head of him whom he had expected so long.

" Father ! " he breathed to himself, and he stood gazing after the chaise till it had passed round another curve and the last gleam of the lights had disappeared. " Pst ! " he whispered. " Bunny ! Did you see that ! "

There was no reply, not a sound but the faint whirr of the wheels growing fainter moment by moment, and, confident now that he could not be seen, the boy left the shelter of the trees, crossed the road, and entered those on the other side beyond the broad strip of grass.

" Bunny ! " he whispered again with no result, and then three times over at intervals he hazarded the call of an owl ; but in vain

Then, after hurrying for a short distance in the direction he felt that his companions must have taken, he was brought up short in a clump of brambles, and, feeling the madness of attempting to follow farther, he began to think.

" I must trust to Bunny getting him safely off, whether I will or not," he muttered. " Oh, but he's sure to get him aboard, and I had not reckoned on this. Father is up at the porch door by now, to find the soldiers searching the place, and the first thing he will say will be, ' Where is Waller ? ' "

The next minute the boy was trotting steadily back towards the Manor, trusting more to instinct than to sight in avoiding the trees.

" And I never said good-bye ! " he kept on muttering. " I never said good-bye ! "

Then all at once he stopped short, panting hard, partly from exertion, partly from excitement, for the thought came strong upon him now of his father.

" He will ask me," he panted, " where I have been ; and what am I to say ? "

An end to the boy's musings was put by the returning post-chaise, whose wheels he heard far ahead, and as soon as it had passed he hurried on along the road ; but before he had gone far he took to cover again, for voices were approaching him in the darkness, one of which, loud and threatening, Waller recognised at once as that of the sergeant in command of the search-party.

He was talking in a menacing tone, and the reply came in a husky, petulant voice, plainly that of the village constable, while directly after there was a chorus of laughter.

Waller shrank farther back amongst the trees, and stood thinking much of his friend's escape, of this second fruitless mission of the soldiery, but, above all, of that which was before him, for, as he hurried on, there, straight before him, his father's stern countenance seemed to rise out of the darkness to look at him with questioning eyes.

The rest of the journey back he saw nothing, heard nothing, thought of nothing, but that stern, questioning face. In fact, later on it seemed to the lad as if there had been a blank until he found himself standing in the well-lit dining-room, listening to his father's words.

These were very few, the principal being comprised in the question, very shortly and sharply uttered—

" Well, Waller, my boy, where have you been ? "

The next minute the tired traveller was sitting back in the big armchair, his brow resting upon one hand, which shaded his face from the young speaker, who slowly, and without a moment's hesitation, spoke out frankly and related all that has been told here.

" Well." said the Squire, as his son ended his narrative, " I am a magistrate, my boy, and it would have been my duty if I had been here to give up that lad to those who sought him.   I was not here, and you acted upon the promptings of your own breast.   Well, my boy, I have had a long and slow journey down ; I am very tired, and I was not pre-pared for such a business as this.   It is late, and beyond your time for bed ; quite mine, too.   And so this young French Englishman whom you have sheltered is on his way with that fellow Wrigg to Loo Creek, where he is to join a lugger, and be set ashore at Cher-bourg ? "

" Yes, father.   But you will not send the soldiers in chase of him now ? "

" Not to-night, my boy," was the reply. " for I am too worn out and weary for anything but bed. I will sleep upon it and see what I think is my duty on the subject to-morrow morning."

" Ah," thought Waller Froy, as he went slowly up, candle in hand, to the room from which his prisoner had so lately escaped ; and his first act was to pick up the jacket Godfrey Boyne had thrown upon the floor.

" Why, I needn't have minded," said Waller to himself. " It's my jacket that I lent him ; and I feel so comfortable and easy now that dad knows all. There, I believe I can sleep better to-night than I have for a month.

He descended to his bedroom, feeling rather sad, though, as he thought of his late companion's journey through the darkness of the night.

Then, as he slowly undressed and laid his head upon the pillow, he had one more wandering thought :

" Will father do anything more about that poor fellow Boyne ? "

The next minute Waller Froy had ceased to think, and thought no more till he opened his eyes upon the light of another bright autumn morning.

" Father said he would sleep upon it.

What will he say to me when we meet ? "
And then another question flashed through
his brain : " France isn't so very far away ;
I wonder whether Godfrey Boyne and I will
ever meet again ? "

www.ingramcontent.com/pod-product-compliance
Lightning Source LLC
Chambersburg PA
CBHW030554040726
47497CB00008B/2716